Niles turned Rose   e
in her pliant body.   ght from the ballroom,
ablaze with candles, filtered through to show her face.
"Why did you say I shouldn't have come? Who do you
think I am?"

"I know who you are." Her whisper was as husky as
his. It seemed to play along his nerves like brushing
feathers. "You're the Black Mask. Have you come to
steal?"

"Yes, that's why I came."

"Tonight? But Mrs. Yarborough is wearing her best
necklace. I saw it."

"A necklace? No, not that." He lifted his hand and
unfastened the tiny jeweled pin that secured her veil.
The smooth silk slipped off the shining satin of her
hair. She pushed her hair behind her ear, looking up
at him with sweet confusion, her lips parted as though
on a word she didn't speak.

"I came for this," he said, holding up the pin. "And
for this."

Niles knew what he wanted was wrong, but he
couldn't resist this attraction any longer. He cupped
her face in his hands, searching her expression for
any sign of what she wanted. Her eyes shone. She slid
her hands over his, slipping them slowly up his
sleeves.

Even Niles couldn't tell which of them kissed first.
He only knew he had a vibrant woman in his arms
who, though obviously inexperienced, possessed all
the depths of passion he'd been longing for. . . .

BOOK YOUR PLACE ON OUR WEBSITE AND MAKE THE READING CONNECTION!

We've created a customized website just for our very special readers, where you can get the inside scoop on everything that's going on with Zebra, Pinnacle and Kensington books.

When you come online, you'll have the exciting opportunity to:

- View covers of upcoming books

- Read sample chapters

- Learn about our future publishing schedule (listed by publication month *and author*)

- Find out when your favorite authors will be visiting a city near you

- Search for and order backlist books from our online catalog

- Check out author bios and background information

- Send e-mail to your favorite authors

- Meet the Kensington staff online

- Join us in weekly chats with authors, readers and other guests

- Get writing guidelines

- AND MUCH MORE!

**Visit our website at
http://www.kensingtonbooks.com**

THE BLACK MASK

Cynthia Pratt

ZEBRA BOOKS
KENSINGTON PUBLISHING CORP.
http://www.kensingtonbooks.com

ZEBRA BOOKS are published by
Kensington Publishing Corp.
850 Third Avenue
New York, NY 10022

All Kensington titles, imprints and distributed lines are available at special quantity discounts for bulk purchases for sales
promotion, premiums, fund-raising, educational or institu-
tional use.

Special book excerpts or customized printings can also be
created to fit specific needs. For details, write or phone the
office of the Kensington Special Sales Manager: Kensington Publishing Corp., 850 Third Avenue, New York, NY
10022. Attn. Special Sales Department. Phone: 1-800-221-
2647.

Zebra and the Z logo Reg. U.S. Pat. & TM Off.

First Printing: January 2003
10 9 8 7 6 5 4 3 1

Printed in the United States of America

To my family

Especially dedicated to
Miss Beth DiSciullo
who has everything she needs to be a writer:
imagination, determination, and love of books.

One

"I hope this won't take the entire day," Rupert said, pacing across the worn carpet of the solicitor's office.

"I'm sure it won't, once Mr. Crenshaw finds those papers." His sister perched on the edge of a rather rickety chair whose once plush velvet covering was now leaking feathers. Every time Rose moved, a little puff of white down shot into the dusty air. Whatever gifts Mr. Crenshaw had as a legal mind, his housekeeping tended toward the negligently casual. Books slid and slipped on tables and shelves, like cliffs suffering serious erosion. Rupert had already caused one avalanche by an incautiously wide turn.

"Your godfather must have been an uncommon eccentric old boy to have such a curst odd lawyer."

"He was out of England for a very long time, Rupert. Perhaps when Mr. Crenshaw was young, he was more sharp-witted."

Rose wished Rupert would sit down, since watching him pace was making her seasick. He had been unusually restless the last several weeks, ever since they'd heard her long-absent godfather had left her a legacy. She had not liked to ask him, but she was very much afraid he'd been gaming and losing again. He'd tell her soon enough if it were true.

"Father said Mr. MacElroy did not meet with good fortune in India."

"Just because the old boy didn't write once he reached the East don't mean he was a failure. Father always looks on the dark side, you know."

"Yes, he is melancholic. But I don't want to indulge hope too far. He might have left me no more than a second silver cup to match the first."

Rupert shook his dark head. "Not even such a queer nabs as this Crenshaw fellow could call a silver cup a legacy. I hope MacElroy's left you a fortune, little Rose. I'd like to see you as rich as Golden Ball." She couldn't doubt the sincerity with which he spoke. Rose only wished she had been left a fortune. She would pay off her younger brother's debts and buy him the commission his father steadfastly refused to give him.

Gavelison MacElroy had been her father's best friend at university. He had stayed in England only long enough to act as godfather to William Spenser's firstborn child. He discharged his duty to the tune of a silver christening cup, vanished to India, and had not been heard of again until a report of his death reached his old friend. Shortly after, the attorney Crenshaw had written to the Spensers regarding a legacy for Rose.

Since Rose and Rupert had planned to go to London on a long-delayed visit to their mother's sister, Mr. Crenshaw thought it best if they deal with the matter in town.

As the minutes ticked past, even Rose became impatient. "Look to see what is keeping him," she urged Rupert.

"All right. I don't mind." Rupert turned toward the door, put his hand to the knob, then let it fall. "Look now, I can't go wandering about yelping for him like a lost pup, can I?"

"I thought you were in a hurry."

"Fact is, I promised to meet some good fellows for a bit of fun and gig. Don't care to disappoint Forbush and Quayle. Top o' the Trees, sticklers for conduct."

"Then you'd better find Mr. Crenshaw," Rose said, though her heart sank at hearing the names of his two most profligate friends. Sons of wealth and privilege, they thought nothing of dropping a few hundred at the tables. Rupert, though the son of a well-to-do banker, couldn't afford to play so deep, especially after his disastrous losses last year.

"Dashed if I will," Rupert said. "I'll no sooner poke my nose out the door than the fellow'll come back. You'll see."

"Heavens!" Followed by further puffs of feathers, Rose went herself. Halfway down the dark hallway, lined with a musty carpet, she passed a door that stood slightly ajar. Someone moved against the light, casting a shadow that flickered in the opening.

"Mr. Crenshaw?" Rose said, pushing open the door. For a moment, she was reminded of the first volume of a Gothic novel she'd read. Her mother had confiscated the other two as soon as she had investigated what Rose was reading.

But no corpses fell into the hall, nor did mad monks pursue her. "Yes? What is it?"

To Rose's mind, an animated skeleton or lurching beast would have been preferable. "Oh, it's you," she said.

"At your service, Miss Spenser."

The dark-haired gentleman of fashion looked out of place behind a desk, long sheets of foolscap scat-

tered before him. The light in the room came over his
shoulder from a half-open window, so Rose could not
see his face well. But she knew that cool, slow, and,
above all, ironic voice.

"Sir Niles. I am surprised to see you here." She
seemed to meet him everywhere she went these days.
Even her bedroom window looked into the garden
at the rear of his house in town.

"Not so surprised as I, Miss Spenser. Mr. Crenshaw
has been my man of affairs for many years, but only
rarely can he interest me in the details of my fortune."

"So long as your gift with cards continues, you
surely need never worry about your fortune," Rose
said tartly.

"A gypsy witch once told me I had lucky hands." Sir
Niles came around the desk. Rose took an involuntary
step back. He wasn't in any way threatening. In fact,
she rather despised him for his dandified ways, yet
some deep feminine instinct warned her against coming within his orbit. Or perhaps it was simply the
memory of all the salacious gossip which circulated
about him.

"Quite a few lucky hands, if my brother tells me
true. He says you never lose."

"Mr. Spenser should learn not to repeat the gossip
of the gaming hells to his sister."

"I'll inform him of your opinion, shall I? He's down
the hall, waiting for Mr. Crenshaw."

"Indeed? And you are not waiting for him?"

Rose told herself she need not answer. If gossip
were true, Sir Niles Alardyce was far too accustomed
to having women do his bidding. Yet politeness demanded she speak. "Mr. Crenshaw has been gone for
some little time. My brother has an engagement
which will not wait."

Sir Niles chuckled coolly. One could not imagine him doing anything so uncouth as laughing out loud. "Knowing Crenshaw as I do, he may very well be standing in some corner with his nose in a law book, tracing some chance thought to its place of origin. For a clever lawyer, he's the most unworldly of men. He has undoubtedly forgotten all about you and your business. I would flatter myself that I am not forgotten were I not quite sure I have been. It must have been half an hour since he left me."

"You tolerate such neglect?" Rose asked as he herded her back to her brother.

"Crenshaw is most astute when it comes to business. My father relied on him totally. Other members of my family have not found him wanting, either."

She noticed, as if for the first time, that Sir Niles was only a few inches taller than she was, perhaps five-foot-eight or -nine. His biscuit-colored waistcoat and Inexpressibles lent the illusion of height under his beautiful blue coat. More than that, however, he carried himself as though he were surveying the earth like a property he considered purchasing.

His haughtiness brought out the urchin in her. Every time she saw him, she felt an unladylike urge to find a nicely squishy beetroot or vegetable marrow to throw at him. She found herself squinting slightly, gauging the distance she'd have to throw a mudball to knock off his ever-so-precisely adjusted hat. She fought the feeling strenuously, knowing it wasn't like her at all. Even as a girl, she'd never done anything so crude. Well, hardly ever. . . .

Rupert turned with a start as Rose and Sir Niles entered. "Alardyce?" he said, an embarrassed blush climbing into his cheeks. Always a handsome boy, his bright complexion showed every feeling, making him look both younger and more innocent than he was. "About those vowels of mine . . ."

Rose saw the chastening glance the man of the world gave Rupert. "No need to worry about that now, Spenser." With the exquisite yet distant manners that marked him, Sir Niles eased Rose into her chair. The fact that she did not, at that moment, wish to sit down seemed less important than giving way to his politeness.

Since she and Rupert had arrived in London, they'd been participating in the social gala that was the Season. Their aunt, Lady Marlton, moved in the first circles of society, though whether because of her youthful widowhood or despite it was a question Rose had not yet solved.

Sir Niles, wealthy, unmarried, and elegant, was a prize every hostess yearned for and every mama prayed for. His reputation for resistance to all female wiles had approached the legendary. The mamas' innocent and not-so-innocent daughters spread snares for his feet, which he avoided with miraculous grace.

"Oh, he's so polite," one of Rose's new friends had complained. "He doesn't notice anything you do, right or wrong, because it wouldn't be polite. It's like dancing with someone who isn't really there."

So Rose had discovered when he had, very politely, begged the favor of a dance with her. His steps were correct and in the proper order. But the whole performance lacked spontaneity or any sense that a dance could be something other than a rather dull social duty. Heaven knew she didn't expect every man who danced with her to flirt, but some demonstration of enjoyment was usual. But no sparkle had awakened in the half-open blue eyes

She decided then he was as cold as a fresh mackerel

and excused herself from the second dance in the set.
Since then, they'd met at other evenings. He had
never again asked her to dance. And yet sometimes
when kicking off her shoes at the end of the evening,
Rose would realize how often she'd turn around and
find him somewhere near.

"I trust your business is not too pressing, Sir Niles,"
Rose asked.

"Oh, I shall happily surrender my appointment to
your claims. No bad news, I hope?"

Rupert gave his rather loud laugh. "I should say
not. Little Rose had a rich godfather, you see. Left her
a fortune."

"Rupert," Rose said, admonishing him with a slight
frown. "We don't know that."

"There's no point in all this folderol if he didn't,"
Rupert said. "Stands to reason a man doesn't go to
lashings of trouble just to hand on a trumpery silver
cup."

"I fear I intrude," Sir Niles said.

"No, no," Rupert said bluffly even as Rose was fram-
ing some polite answer that meant 'yes, you do.'

"I quite understand."

Rose felt he had somehow read her mind and knew
exactly how reluctant she was to have him near her.

Sir Niles looked past Rupert and smiled broadly.
Rose blinked a little, surprised by the flash of warmth
from his suddenly brilliant blue eyes. She turned to
look toward the door. Mr. Crenshaw had returned.

"Oh. Here you are, Sir Niles. I found the reference
to the statute of limitations. It seems that in a case
such as . . ."

"I beg your pardon, Mr. Crenshaw," Rose said
loudly and clearly. "This gentleman has kindly allowed us the first opportunity of consulting with you."

"Oh, indeed. Very kind of Sir Niles, always kind. Now, young lady, what can I do for you?"

The attorney didn't look as absentminded as his behavior led one to believe. He wore neat dark clothes with no extravagances, was somewhere in his middle fifties, with beautifully combed iron-gray hair, and his only distinguishing characteristic was that he constantly rubbed his thumb over the back case of his watch. Rose had already noticed the slight groove he'd worn into the gold.

Only his eyes gave his vagueness away. They never rested on one object or person very long without roaming. It was as if his eyes were in constant need of fresh sights. Now he blinked slowly at Rose.

"Don't you remember?" she asked.

"Ah, yes," he said with a smile. "A marriage contract, wasn't it? This gentleman is going to act for you? You must be of age, you know."

"I am of age. And we're here regarding Mr. MacElroy's estate."

"You're of age?" Mr. Crenshaw asked, with doubtful lines on his brow.

Rose sighed and tried to remember it was rude to roll one's eyes. "I am twenty-two," she said for the second time today. In attempt to forestall a repetition of his questions, she volunteered what she'd told Mr. Crenshaw the first time. "I should have come to London several years ago to make my debut, but first my mother fell ill and then we went into mourning for my grandmother."

"But your mother is well?"

"Quite well, Mr. Crenshaw. Now, about Mr. MacElroy's legacy?" She could feel Rupert's impatience with the older man's doddering ways. He no longer troubled to hide his increasing yawns.

"Ah, yes. Mr. MacElroy. A fine man, but a wild spirit. I have his last letter somewhere." He slid open the top drawer of his desk and rummaged a minute. "Perhaps it's in a file. I should be able to put my hand on it in a moment or so."

"I should be most interested to see it, sir. However, my brother has an engagement this afternoon, and I don't want to impose upon Sir Niles's good temper for too long."

"My time is yours, Miss Spenser," Sir Niles said. Was it her dislike of him that seemed to color his every comment with irony? Or was it the way his eyes were always half closed, heavy lids weighted down with thick lashes, as though he spent his life half asleep or half hidden?

Rose wondered why that image had occurred to her. Half hidden? Surely Sir Niles hid nothing. His escapades were well known, even notorious, though she asked herself how so indolent a man could have found the energy for questionable pursuits.

"Nevertheless," she said, "if we could expedite this matter . . ."

"Certainly, certainly," Mr. Crenshaw said, absently patting his pockets. "There's the matter of the receipt and, of course, the inspection. Shan't take but a moment more." His patting hands slowed. "Oh, dear, now what did I do with it?"

Rose prided herself on the evenness of her temper. In a household where her father brooded, her mother enjoyed ill health, and her brother was prey to a restlessness that invariably plunged him into trouble, she was constrained to be coolheaded. All too often, the responsibility for a smoothly run household devolved onto her. She liked to think she handled the matters that fell within her compass with skill and poise, but she had no authority over a doddering old man. As for Sir Niles, how he would make game of her if she lost her temper.

Fortunately for her reputation, Mr. Crenshaw thought of looking in the top drawer of his battered desk. "Here it is," he crowed.

He laid out a long sheet of paper and a small box carved from some reddish wood accented with brass. A faint scent, exotic and strange, wended through the dusty, book-flavored air. For the first time, Rose felt a flutter of excitement. What had her mysterious god-father left to her?

Sir Niles cleared his throat softly. "I shall wait outside the door if you require my services, Miss Spenser."

"You are very kind, sir, but I think we can dispense with your services. No doubt Mr. Crenshaw's clerk can assist us if any papers require a signature."

"As you wish, ma'am. Good afternoon, Spenser."

"Eh? Oh, quite. 'Til this evening, eh?" Rupert hastened to open the door for his friend. Returning, he threw himself petulantly into the other chair. A small puff of feathers came out like punctuation. "Rose, you don't talk to Sir Niles Alardyce like that," he hissed in an angry undertone.

"And how did I speak to him?"

"Like you prefer a dashed clerk's services to his. As if he don't matter."

"I assure you he doesn't matter. Not to me."

"But . . . but he's Sir Niles Alardyce," he said, almost in a panic at her female incomprehension. "Dash it. He invented the St. George lapel. He bested the Prince Regent's time to Brighton. He brought *caramel au chocolat* into fashion."

"Admirable as all his gifts may be," Rose said, "I

hardly think any of them qualify him to be privy to my private affairs." She turned toward Mr. Crenshaw. "I beg your pardon, sir. If you would care to proceed?"

For a moment, a gleam of a great and kindly intelligence appeared in Mr. Crenshaw's eyes, twinkling at her from behind his rimless glasses. "I had a younger brother myself, Miss Spenser."

He cleared his throat and became the perfect lawyer. "This is the last will and testament of Mr. Gavelison MacElroy. 'Being of sound mind and body, and with a due regard for the mercy of heaven which I pray to receive in my life hereafter, I declare this to be my final will . . .'"

Mr. Crenshaw read on in his thin voice. Rupert leaned forward, his hands dangling loosely between his knees as he concentrated on the involved sentences and legal language of the will. After a few minutes, however, the rolling sentences seemed to overwhelm him. He leaned back in his chair, adopting a more relaxed posture. His brown eyes, so like her own, became glazed as his jaw slackened. Soon he was yawning.

Rose confessed she shared her brother's confusion. Most of the will seemed to concern itself with individual bequests to servants and friends in India. She heard strange names and tried to picture, for example, what a statue of Lord Ganesha or Lord Hanuman must look like. She had no difficulty at all imagining her father's reaction if a cartload of Indian curiosities arrived at Berling Manor and hoped her godfather had not left her any of his collection.

Rupert's head had begun to nod when the words, "and to my beloved goddaughter, Rose Redcliffe Spenser, I devise and bequeath" snapped his eyes open.

"What's that?"

Mr. Crenshaw increased the volume of his mumble. "The sum of one hundred pounds and the jewel known as the Malikzadi."

"A jewel, b'Jove!" Rupert exclaimed, sitting bolt upright.

"What does it mean, Mr. Crenshaw? Mal . . . *malikzadi*?"

"I believe it means *queen,* Miss Spenser. How the ruby came by that name, Mr. MacElroy did not divulge."

He reached out with his dry hand and twisted the key in the front of the sandalwood box. The lid opened slowly, as if by clockwork.

Drawn forward without realizing it, Rose left her chair to peer into the velvet-lined depths. "Oh."

"Stand aside, old girl." Rupert flipped the lid fully open with his thumb. "By George! Is that it?"

Reaching in to grasp the contents, he suddenly pulled his fingers back. "I say!" he exclaimed, shaking his hand vigorously. "Something bit me!"

Two

"Rupert!" Rose started forward, her heart like a cold lump in her breast.

Rupert looked at his hand curiously, turning it palm up. "No, it's all right. Not a mark on me. But I swear . . ."

"Ah," the attorney said, taking up the box. "I neglected to set the thief catcher back. Very clever device," he added, twisting a small section of inlaid brass. "It seems the former owner liked to smear poison on a blade set into this little swinging arm. Should anyone attempt to steal the contents, the blade would cut the thief's hand."

"And you let my brother . . . Rupert, are you certain you're not hurt?"

"Devil a scratch, Rose. Don't fuss. I'm sure the blade has been taken out. Hasn't it, Mr. Crenshaw?"

For a heart-stopping instant, Mr. Crenshaw crinkled his brow and studied the ceiling. "Oh, yes, certainly. That is . . . yes, certainly. There's nothing to fear. Come and see."

With some trepidation, Rose took the richly ornamented box in her hand. When she opened it fully, the sight within wiped away the memory of her brother's near miss.

Cut like a pyramid, the strawberry-red ruby jutted

up from a nest of purple-shaded smaller rubies. Though of impressive size, as big as the top joint of Rupert's thumb, the depths of the main stone were foggy, the color weakened by a white web of inclusions. As every stone was set in bright yellow gold, all the colors clashed instead of mingling. Rose had never seen anything so ugly. It was as if some craftsman had set himself the task of making the most hideous piece of jewelry possible. And it was hers, all hers.

"What's it worth?" Rupert asked.

"I have no information about that, Mr. Spenser. Of course, your sister should have some competent authority appraise the jewel as soon as possible. Rundell and Bridge, for example. Or, if you wish to know at once, Sir Niles has a very fine understanding of precious stones. I believe they have been his hobby for several years."

"Aren't you going to try it on?" Rupert urged.

Rose took the ring from its faded velvet slot. It slipped on easily, too easily. Whoever had owned the Malikzadi before must have had the hands of a prizefighter. By pressing her fingers together, she could keep the ring on the top of her hand instead of slipping around to her palm. It seemed to squat on her middle finger like a warty red toad.

"It's not very practical for day wear," she said.

Her brother laughed shortly. "Speaking for myself, I'd prefer you didn't wear it at all. Great gaudy pieces of jewelry went out with Charles the Second." He stepped to the door. "Let's have Alardyce in. He's an expert, you know, and we could do worse."

"No, Rupert," Rose said, but not quickly enough.

It seemed Sir Niles would be only too happy to serve the Spensers by looking at the Malikzadi. Before Rose could slip the ring off, he took her fingers in his and bowed over the ring. His fingers were warm and dry, his nails beautifully kept. Though his touch achieved the impersonal, the continuation of his hold made Rose feel oddly trapped. With a strong tug, she freed her fingers, leaving the ring in his possession. He brought out his quizzing glass for closer inspection.

"Indian manufacture, of course. Probably cut in Bombay. Very finely cut, even the smallest stones. Twenty-four-karat gold, which accounts for the color. The beadwork between each stone is really quite remarkable."

"So it's valuable," Rupert said, peering eagerly over Sir Niles's shoulder.

"A few hundred pounds, perhaps, to a collector."

"Such as yourself, Sir Niles," Rose said, narrowing her eyes.

"Not at all, Miss Spenser. I possess all I desire of the Indian ruby. No, the poor color and clarity condemns it. A pity, as otherwise the size and cutting of the stone would recommend it. So much effort wasted over so poor a specimen."

"Well there's one good thing to remember," Rupert said, with the air of one who can find good in any situation. "At least the Black Mask won't come calling on you, Rose."

"The Black Mask?" she repeated.

"Spenser, there's no need to frighten your sister," Sir Niles said, his drawling voice sharpening.

"Oh, I'm not afraid," Rose said. Was there a maiden in London who hadn't secretly thrilled to hear the whispered tale of the daring thief no lock could stop? The Countess of Hopewood had awakened to find a huge figure of a man, clad all in black, rifling her dressing case. When pressed on why she did not scream for help, the countess had confessed to believing that she dreamed, for surely no mortal man could be so massive. The count had not been pleased.

"You have more cause to be frightened than I, Sir Niles. I hope your jewel collection is in a safe place."

"I keep those items too precious to lose in a locked box under my bed, Miss Spenser. No thief would think to look there."

"Perhaps not. But the Black Mask seems a most unusual thief."

Two nights ago, the house of a man grown hugely rich on cotton manufacture had been raided and his newly purchased and very vulgar diamond-headed cane had been stolen. The thief wasn't seen, though a beggar, sitting on a curb, later gave witness that a black shadow had stooped over him and left the countess's emerald diadem in his lap. Not knowing how to turn such a piece into cash money, he turned it in at Bow Street, collecting a considerable reward.

The Black Mask, it seemed, had a passion for equality, as well as for jewelry.

"Have you heard the latest?" Rupert asked of no one in particular.

"What is it?" Rose forgot to be cold and blasé in front of Sir Niles.

"That fellow he robbed—Curtis, was it?"

"Curtman," Sir Niles supplied.

"That's it. Curtman. Turns out the fellow was nothing but a cursed slave trader, selling the poor devils to plantation owners. Had any number of ships moving, all the while pretending to ship cotton. They say he'll be up before the beak come tomorrow, and dashed well serves him right." He glared around as though daring anyone to contradict him. "I know this Black

Mask fellow is nothing but a common thief, but this time I say jolly well done!"

"But what did the Black Mask have to do with Mr. Curtman's slaving?" Rose asked.

Mr. Crenshaw obligingly answered. "The, er, gentleman in question was unwise enough to entrust to a secret strongbox his collection of accounts pertaining to the acquiring of his fortune. It seems in the course of his other activities, the thief discovered this cache."

"How?" Rose asked, agog.

"It's believed one of Curtman's servants must have betrayed the secret, though they all deny it stridently."

"There, you see, Sir Niles," Rose said triumphantly. "If he could find this person's secret lockbox, he could find yours."

"Very true. I shall invent a new hiding place at once."

"Tell her who got the papers," Rupert said, chuckling, as he drew out his snuff box. He didn't wait for Mr. Crenshaw. "The prime minister!"

"The prime minister?"

Mr. Crenshaw coughed, disapprovingly. "The incriminating documents were, so it seems, laid under Lord Liverpool's eyes at breakfast when his butler attempted to pour him a cup of tea. There was no tea in the pot, only the papers. A deplorable thing to happen at breakfast. They say poor Lord Liverpool suffered from indigestion the rest of the day."

"However did the Black Mask put the papers into the teapot?" Rose asked, smiling at Mr. Crenshaw's belief in the sacredness of breakfast.

"No one knows that either," he said. "But it does show that the fellow in question suffers from a rather juvenile sense of humor."

"Of course," Sir Niles said, "slavery itself is not yet illegal. Only the actual trafficking in slaves."

Rose turned cool eyes upon him. She had no wish to be fair to Mr. Curtman, and thought it very like Sir Niles to see the immoral side of what was a very plain issue.

"An excellent point, Sir Niles," Mr. Crenshaw said. "And this Curtman was clever enough not to transport his slaves in ships of British registry. Nonetheless, I think even if he should escape fining—which, at a hundred pounds a head for each slave mentioned in his very complete records, is no bagatelle—Mr. Curtman will find life most unpleasant in London."

Rupert sneezed and laughed at the same time, a bizarre sound. "To be sure," he said, bringing out an overlarge handkerchief. "There's not a hostess will receive him, and his marriage to Miss Stonebridge has been broken off."

"The daughter of 'Liberator' Stonebridge?" Rose asked. "I met her only last week. She's a sweet, sweet girl."

"She's better off," Rupert said, sneezing. "This Curtman was giving money to the antislavery cause with one hand while making money from slaves with the other hand. That's the kind of hypocrisy we fought the French over, and here it is right in London. Why, the very thought makes me want to shout!"

"Poor Miss Stonebridge."

"She's better off," Rupert repeated. "If it were you, Rose, being made up to by such a cursed hypocrite, I'd hang the fellow before I'd let him marry you. The Black Mask did the girl a good turn."

"I'm sure she'll come to see that in time," Mr. Crenshaw said. "Now, er, regarding your inheritance . . ."

"Oh, yes," Rose said, embarrassed that they'd wandered so far from the point. "We are, I'm afraid, wasting a great deal of your time, sir, over a very minor matter."

"Not at all, Miss Spenser. Besides," he said with what in another person would have been a mischievous glance over his spectacles, "it is Sir Niles's time."

Rose, willing to acknowledge when she was in the wrong, offered Sir Niles her hand once more. "I apologize, Sir Niles. You have been more than kind."

"A pleasure to be of service. May I?" He slipped the side of his hand under her sensitive fingertips. She felt her face heat. She'd held hands with men during dances a hundred times or more, but something about the way Sir Niles touched her seemed strangely intimate. Surely it must be all on her side, since his eyes remained cool and remote while he slid the Malikzadi on her middle finger. Besides, he would never do anything so impolite as flirt. "Rundell and Bridge would be happy, no doubt, to make it fit your finger comfortably."

"Oh, I shall never wear it. I am not fond of rubies— or indeed of any jewelry. I wear pearls."

"One day perhaps you will change your mind. Only a woman can bring out the true beauty of a fine stone."

"I like pearls," she said, determined to be contrary. She gave him a too bright smile. "Thank you again, Sir Niles, for your assistance and your opinion."

"Both are always at your service," he said, bowing.

Rose hated how Sir Niles always contrived to have the last word. She could hardly concentrate on the rest of Mr. Crenshaw's legalities as she tried to think of something polite but crushing to say to Sir Niles the next time they met.

Half an hour later, when the Spensers had gone, Sir Niles entered Mr. Crenshaw's office again. The attorney looked up from his endless paperwork. "Are you satisfied, my boy?"

"I confess I feel better." Sir Niles, his affectations laid aside for the moment, dropped into the chair recently occupied by Rose Spenser. He smiled at the exhalation of fluff even as he leaned his head back. Sprawling there, the attorney could see the lines of fatigue under his eyes and the pale, almost transparent skin at the temple.

"You may feel better, Niles, but you look like the devil. Did you sleep at all last night?"

"No. I was a trifle busy." Gone was the drawling, ironic voice. He spoke crisply, his words falling quickly from his lips. "The rooftops of London are not made for swift or easy travel. But that is where my path lies."

"Surely you'll stop now. Curtman is finished. Beringer is proving very hard to catch. As for the other . . ."

Shaking off his exhaustion like a dog coming out of a lake, Niles sat up, looking as alert and bright as though he'd had a blissful night's sleep. "He's as guilty as they are. I won't let him escape. No, and not Beringer either. He left a letter for me. He's ready to swallow the hook."

Mr. Crenshaw leaned forward, trying to force Niles to look at him. But the younger man dug his finger into one of the slits in the ancient fabric of the chair, enlarging the hole, his entire attention apparently consumed in the task. "There's no proof in his case. No weaknesses like Curtman's record. No bait to use as in Beringer's case."

"I can think of one way to trap him."

"Niles." Mr. Crenshaw managed at last to make Niles look up. The blue eyes regarded him with affection, but Crenshaw knew how easily that blue gaze could set into intractability as hard as flint. He'd known Niles Alardyce from boyhood and he had al-

ways been just the same. Easygoing, kindly, gentle-
manly, but capable of a resolution second to none.
Not even those he loved best could alter his purpose
once he'd decided on a course of action. Only his
mother, perhaps, and she had died too young.

"Niles, I can't help you anymore," Crenshaw said,
using the only weapon he had against that iron will.
"This business with the prime minister, that cuts too
near the bone. If they'd caught you, they would have
shot you as a suspected assassin. The scandal . . ."

"He was the only one who'd expose Curtman piti-
lessly. The others would want to take care of him
quietly. Liverpool's no Wellington, but he knows right
from wrong."

"I won't help you get yourself killed."

"I sympathize, Crenshaw."

"You'll stop, then? Stop with Beringer."

Niles shook his head. The confident expression he
wore worried Crenshaw. He'd seen it too many times,
and it always presaged heart palpitations in anyone
who became entangled in one of Niles's schemes.
Niles never seemed to feel any qualms. He left those
to other people. Niles had only ever worried about
one person. Was, it seemed, still worried about him
even now.

"Christian wouldn't want you to risk your life for a
quixotic quest."

Niles laughed shortly. "He'd be the first to urge me
on to greater folly, Crenshaw, and you know it. Next
to Christian, I always looked like a demmed respectable citizen."

"I cannot persuade you to give it up?"

Niles shook his head, but seemed more interested
in extracting one feather at a time than in answering
his man of affairs's questions.

The attorney sighed and changed the subject. "A charming young couple, the Spensers," he said. "The boy is a trifle immature."

"No more so than some others I could name. Like most young men on their first visit to London, he has a certain amount to learn. A pity the lessons so often come at a price."

"He gambles?"

"Incessantly. And badly."

"From what he said, I infer you hold some of his debts?"

"Almost all of them."

"May I ask why?"

"Better me than a Captain Sharp. There are many who see such a fellow as no more than pigeon for plucking."

"You have taken him under your wing, then. Why him in particular? There are a great many young country fellows in the city at any time. You've never shown any interest in protecting their feathers from plucking."

Niles flicked at few feathers at the attorney. "Perhaps he reminds me of the son I never had," he said flippantly.

"Or the brother-in-law?" the attorney suggested slyly.

Crenshaw congratulated himself on surprising the unflappable Sir Niles. For a moment, the brilliant blue eyes stared at him, frozen. Then the handsome, high-nosed face thawed as a chuckle broke from his lips. "Is it that I am being obvious?"

"I have known you a very long time. May I say I am glad to see you are considering doing your duty by your name and rank?" Crenshaw wanted to express his relief that Niles still had a heart, but there were some subjects one did not raise with a client, however long guarded and well loved.

"You go too fast. Miss Spenser is the merest acquaintance; nothing more."

"Yet you protect her brother from the consequences of his folly?"

"Someone has to. He's not equipped for the task."

Mr. Crenshaw drummed his fingernails on the desk. "Miss Spenser is a very lovely girl."

"Yes, I suppose she is. I, however, admire Miss Spenser for her independence of mind. She is one of the few who have not fallen under Sir Niles's rather stuffy spell."

"She doesn't like you."

"She doesn't like Sir Niles. She has never met me."

Three

"I simply don't understand you, Rose. Everybody *else* likes Sir Niles."

One thing about Rupert, Rose thought. He was tenacious. Let him grab hold of a subject, and he'd shake it to death like a terrier with a rabbit. "Then he hardly needs my approval."

"But he's really the best of good fellows. Not at all high in the instep."

"I would say that is exactly what he is. Proud, superior, and overweening."

"Just because he isn't falling over himself to set up as one of your flirts."

Rose, heedless of the interested housemaid sweeping the steps, turned sharply toward her more than usually aggravating younger brother as he stepped down from the carriage. "I do not have 'flirts.' Of all the vulgar . . ."

"Please yourself. I suppose Manbridge wasn't flirting with you last night at Lady Welsh's?"

"He was telling me about shooting."

"Is that why he had his arm around your waist? And I suppose that Italian, what's-his-name, was telling you about astronomy in the garden?"

"If you remember, it was very hot last night. Perhaps you didn't notice, busy as you were in the card room."

The housemaid hurried to open the green-painted front door, dropping a curtsy as they passed in. "How are you, Mary?" Rose asked. "Is my aunt in?"

"Healthy as a horse, miss, ta. Her ladyship's in her boudoir." She giggled as Rupert gave her a wink.

"Coming up?" Rose asked him as she unbuttoned the sleeves of her jaconet muslin pelisse. "Aunt Paige will want to hear all the details."

"I'd better change first. I'm dust all over from that office. Can't go out like this." He indicated his disarray with a wave of his hand, but Rose thought he looked very handsome in his tight blue coat and fanciful tie. She at least owed Sir Niles a little gratitude, for, profiting by his example, Rupert had toned down his love for the wilder fields of fashion.

"Will you be out very late tonight, Rupert? I wouldn't ask, only there's a breakfast tomorrow and Mrs. Lane made a special point of asking if you could come."

"Is that spotty daughter of hers going to be there?"

"I imagine she will. It is being given in her honor. And she doesn't have that many spots."

Rupert sighed and kicked lightly at the black and white checked floor of the foyer. "I'll go if you want me to."

"I always enjoy being escorted by handsome men. Didn't you just say so?"

He raised his hand as though he'd strike her. Rose just wrinkled her nose at him. "Don't worry; you won't be called out to defend my honor. If I lose my good name, I'll just drown myself so politely even your precious Sir Niles will approve."

She danced away before he could catch her, laughing. When she put a foot on the bottommost stair, he called her. Hearing a serious note in his voice, she turned back.

"Don't forget your inheritance," he said, reaching out, box in hand.

"Oh, thank you. Aunt Paige will want to see this." Rose looked up into his face. "Do you mind very much that I didn't receive a fortune?"

Rupert could hardly shrug in his tight coat, but he pulled a shrugging kind of face. "A few thousands would have come in dashed opportune. The dibs aren't in tune often these days."

"Bad luck?"

"I wish it were only bad luck. That would be an improvement."

"Rupert . . . I could sell the ring. It's not much, but Sir Niles said it would bring something."

"That's what I mean about your poor taste in men, Rose. You'd throw everything away on a wastrel like me and never look twice at a chap like Sir Niles. He's got the ready in sackfuls, dashed if he doesn't, and the devil's own luck with it."

"You're not a wastrel," Rose said, seizing his arm and shaking it. "If Father would let you join up, you'd be the finest soldier . . ."

"What's the use of talking about it? He'll never let me go. And the war's over, anyway. Maybe your old godfather had it right. India's the place for someone like me. But, by God, I would have liked to see it in the Army."

He pushed past her, taking the stairs two at a time with the air of one who outran his thoughts. Rose followed more slowly. By the time she reached the top, Rupert had gone into his room. The lustily sung and off-key strains of the latest comic song burst forth.

Rose hardly had time to unpin the hat from her head before a light tap on her door heralded her aunt. "May I come in?"

"Of course," Rose said, swinging the door wide. "I'm sorry I didn't come directly to your room, but that office was amazingly dusty."

"Lawyers' offices always are," said Lady Marlton, twice a widow and therefore conversant with the law and lawyers. "I should have warned you not to wear that dark red. It is more than becoming, my love, but it shows every smudge. Turn 'round. Let me unbutton you."

Rose smiled as she turned obediently, bending her knees to bring her topmost button into reach. Her mother's sister was what men called a pocket Venus. Barely five feet tall, she was perfectly proportioned, even though her second widowhood and the boxes of bonbons she consumed to alleviate her boredom had put some weight on her. Or at least she claimed to have been bored.

Since her niece and nephew had come to stay, they had hardly spent two consecutive nights at home. Rose hadn't imagined there could be so many parties. The knocker at Aunt Paige's elegant town house was never silent for long, and though Rose came in for her share of attention, more than a few bouquets and treats had been for the widow. Lady Marlton moved in the first circle of London society, and her friends waited breathlessly to see which of the competing eligible older gentlemen would be her third lord and master.

"Colonel Wapton called while you were out. He was amazingly sorry to have missed you."

"I shall make it up to him with a dance this evening."

"Perhaps you should make him suffer. Along with Mr. March, young Lord Duchan, and the Right Honorable Member from Preffendale."

"Did all those gentlemen call while I was out?"

"Yes, and were like to wear out the furniture. Why must you attract such outsized suitors?"

"They only seem like that to you, Aunt."

"Wicked!"

Rose laughed as she picked up her dressing gown. "Don't you want to see what my godfather did leave me? Besides a hundred pounds."

"A hundred pounds is a hundred pounds," Aunt Paige said consideringly. "Not a fortune, but enough to make a journey into the City worthwhile. But you said *besides* . . . he didn't leave you a plantation or any such thing, did he? Really, you mustn't even think of going to India. A dreadful place, by all I hear. Is that what Rupert was saying in the hall? You children must learn not to have arguments in public. I honestly thought he meant to strike you!"

"Rupert hasn't struck me since he was seven years old, Aunt. Even that was an accident."

Picking up the case, she relished the look of anticipation on her aunt's face. Certainly nothing could prepare her for the wonders of the Malikzadi.

"My word." Aunt Paige laughed a little. "How perfectly ghastly."

"Wonderful thing, isn't it?" Rose slipped it again onto her middle finger.

"It's the ugliest piece of jewelry I ever saw, except for the Queen of Naples's diamond tiara. The woman had no taste. She would have loved that ring."

"If I am ever in Naples, I'll make her a gift of it. It bears the name of a queen."

"Does it? Which one?"

"I mean, it's called Queen. In Indian. *Malikzadi.*" She slipped it off and handed it to her aunt. "It's large enough to make you a bracelet."

"I wouldn't have it as a gift," Aunt Paige said, holding her pretty hands up. "You keep it. Maybe it will be your good luck charm. Did you say it's worthless?"

"Not worthless, precisely. Sir Niles said . . ." She closed her mouth instantly, but wasn't quite quick enough.

"Sir Niles? Sir Niles Alardyce?"

Rose nodded resignedly. Was she to suffer another paean of praise to the incomparable, inimitable, insufferable Sir Niles?

"Whatever was he doing at an attorney's office?"

"He said Mr. Crenshaw had long been his man of affairs."

"Poor man must keep very busy if he is directing Sir Niles's affairs."

Though she was very fond of her socially adept aunt, Rose did not like it when she gave vent to one of her sophisticated little laughs, leaving Rose with the feeling that she was a very ignorant and foolish girl indeed. Many older women laughed like that, with a cynical intonation that made Sir Niles's irony seem like sweet-tempered enthusiasm. She wondered if she would come to laugh like that when she turned forty.

"I confess I don't like Sir Niles very much," she said. "But he doesn't seem like a libertine."

"The most talented ones never do, dear heart. But never mind. Did he see this?" She pointed to the ruby.

"Yes, he examined it."

"And pronounced upon it? A coup! Why, there are ladies by the score who have attempted to entice Sir Niles into looking at their gawds—usually while resting upon their bosoms. That man must have looked into more crevasses than a Swiss mountain guide."

"You like Sir Niles yourself, Aunt."

"I confess I do. There's something about a very cold

man. The challenge, I suppose. Oh, well. He's years and years too young for me."

"Are you going to marry again, Aunt?"

"Inquisitive, aren't you?" Aunt Paige smiled mysteriously and fluttered over to Rose's wardrobe. The room she'd given her niece was far quieter than Rupert's, which looked right onto the street and was filled with noises from the call of the knife grinder to the bone-shaking rumble of delivery wagons drawn by horses with feet the size of pies.

Rose's room looked out over the back garden, a quiet, hardly used space except on sunny days, when the staff would take a few moments to lift their faces, like so many sunflowers, to the rarely glimpsed sky. Rose missed the blue sky over her home. In London, the air was too often tinged with the yellow stains of fog and coal smoke.

In fact, the only drawback to this charming, airy room was that the garden marched down to meet Sir Niles Alardyce's brick wall. His garden, while not as beautifully tended as Paige's, served as a continuation of hers, so Rose had several hundred feet of nearly uninterrupted greenery to admire. She did admire it, except when she looked out her window to see Sir Niles taking the air. Then the view was spoiled.

While Aunt Paige romped happily through her new dresses, Rose sat down to cleanse her face and hands in a basin. "What is going forward tonight, Aunt?"

"The opera, my dear, and then Lady Fitzmonroe has had the most diverting notion. An *indoor* picnic. She's turned her ballroom into a sylvan glade, if you can believe it."

"Sounds charming."

"Complete with a stream! Everyone will be copying her, mark my words."

"And are we all to dress like milkmaids?" Rose asked, drying her face.

"No, no. It's not a masquerade. There hasn't been a decent masquerade yet this year."

"That reminds me. Aunt, have you heard of the Black Mask's latest escapade?"

"You mean the prime minister? Your admirers were full of nothing else. Of course, being men, they all think the Black Mask is nothing but a rogue with imagination."

"What do you think?"

"I?" For a moment, Aunt Paige peeked around the open wardrobe door, her cap askew on her still golden hair. "If I were a young girl again, I should be lost in daydreams of such a dashing fellow. As a staid matron, however, I should naturally deplore the whole business, but I can't quite bring myself to do so." She giggled like a girl. "What do your friends think?"

"That he is Robin Hood come to life again. But I told them one gift to the poor does not a Robin Hood make. Besides, I'm sorry for poor Miss Stonebridge. What a horrible way to find out about your lover."

"Better she should learn now than after they've taken their vows. I understand Mr. Stonebridge has threatened to horsewhip Curtman when he's released from the magistrate's. One of your admirers—they all do look so alike, Rose!—said bets are being taken that Curtman will flee the country. Apparently, no odds are offered he'll do the honorable thing."

"What honorable thing?"

Again Aunt Paige's head popped out. "Suicide," she whispered, like a ghost.

"I wonder if that would make Miss Stonebridge feel better or worse."

"Here," Aunt Paige exclaimed. She stepped into plain view, waving a gown like a flag of triumph. "You shall wear this!"

The cream-colored silk was embroidered all over with green leaves in a shimmering thread. The square neck was outlined in deep green velvet ribbon, which was echoed in a triple row around the hem. "And flowers in your hair. Roses, I think. Pink roses. They'll look vastly sweet peeking from your dark curls." Lady Marlton squinted at her niece, visualizing the prospect. "My dear, you'll charm the birds from the trees."

"Lady Fitzmonroe imported birds for the evening?"

"I shouldn't be at all surprised. She's a frighteningly thorough woman."

As she unpinned her curling hair, Rose thought of Rupert. "Aunt, aren't you going to ask Rupert to escort us?"

"I already did. He's made some engagement with a party of friends. But you needn't worry. I asked Mr. Dickson to be so kind. He'll call for us at eight."

"Mr. Dickson?"

"Forgotten one of your admirers already?" Aunt Paige teased. "Well, with so many of them . . ."

"Which one is he?"

"You met him at Almack's. Tall, slightly graying, about forty, I suppose. He made his fortune in the City, but his mother was a de Matelet. So he's quite eligible."

"Aunt . . ."

Aunt Paige pushed a footstool close to Rose and sank down on it gracefully. "Older men make very secure husbands, my love. A trifle boring, perhaps, but one always knows where they are. But if you prefer the young and dashing, why not take Colonel Wapton?"

"He's not precisely young. He must be as old as your Mr. Dickson."

"But certainly dashing in his uniform."

Rose sighed. She'd known this moment would come and had decided to be both frank and determined. "Aunt, I appreciate your interest on my behalf. But I have no scheme to marry any of these estimable gentlemen."

"Why not?" A slight frown creased her forehead and was instantly rubbed away. "Pray don't tell me you are stuffed full of ridiculous notions about marrying for love."

With becoming meekness, Rose looked away. "I made sure you of all people would be sympathetic to my plight."

But Aunt Paige caught the note of stifled laughter. "You thought nothing of the kind, minx." She pinched Rose's cheek.

Then Rose did laugh aloud. "I can't say I have too many ridiculous notions," she said when she recovered. "But I cannot bring myself to consider marriage only in terms of economics."

"As is only right. A young girl shouldn't consider such matters. Properties, jointures, pin money . . . these things are better left to fathers. Let them sprout gray hairs while the women go mad buying bride clothes."

"I agree. However, I am a banker's daughter and my blood runs true."

Aunt Paige looked curiously at her niece. "Do you wish you had been born a boy so you could have been a banker yourself?"

"Not at all. Being a woman has so many benefits that I can hardly cavil at those inconveniences that go with it." She toyed with her silver-backed hairbrush and comb. "I know perfectly well there is no other suitable path for me but marriage. I don't burn to reform the world, Aunt, but if given a choice, I should like a marriage that is more than a merger of two equal properties."

Aunt Paige shook her head but seemed pleased. "Well, that sounds more practical than foolish. A girl must have her dreams, but she must consider her future very carefully." Aunt Paige patted Rose's knee. "I made up my mind when I invited you to come to London that you'd not go home without a promised husband. Your mother, as you know, cannot interest herself in finding you a husband at this time. If you put it off much longer, you'll be on the shelf through no fault of your own."

"A terrible fate, to be sure."

"Yes, it is. You've no notion."

"After delaying my debut for two years, I have a very good notion indeed. Last year was the dullest of my life. I vowed when I came to London I'd be gay to dissipation, and so I intend."

"Excellent. The best way to find a husband is to search for one. He won't come climbing through your window, you know. Not unless you intend to marry the Black Mask!"

Aunt Paige stayed to gossip and to direct her own maid in the dressing of Rose's hair. Rose nodded and laughed in the right places, but her thoughts were busy. Though she disavowed all romantical fancies, the truth lay somewhere between illusion and reality. She cherished her dreams of finding and marrying a man she could truly love, but had long ago learned not to speak of them. Dreams, she found, withered faster than rosebuds in winter when scorn or rough humor followed their telling.

She liked her indulgent, fashionable aunt very much, yet feared too much exposure to her cynicism would kill her dreams for good and all. Rose didn't believe that she could marry for love alone. Too many kindly and practical people were watching out for her interests. Besides, she would never marry to disoblige her family. She would choose a good, sensible man and hope his admirable qualities would spark the tenderer emotions in her heart just as everyone promised. "Love comes with time," seemed to be the refrain she was to take to heart.

Meanwhile, no one could prevent her dreaming of her hero, some man who dared all odds like a knight of olden days, who would face dragons for his lady and win her heart in the moment of his victory. Rose knew these were only dreams that could never come true, yet they were very sweet. She couldn't surrender them just yet.

Four

Lady Fitzmonroe's inspiration more than fulfilled its promise. Banks of newly opened flowers filled the air of the ballroom with the thousand scents of spring, while the cleverly improvised stream made rippling music in sweet counterpoint to the orchestra. The musicians and, indeed, all the servants were dressed like yeomen, having put off their powered wigs and knee breeches for the evening. The butler wore a disgruntled expression when he'd opened the door, obviously not relishing his smock and trousers.

Rose had danced with half a dozen men before she'd had a moment to herself. She'd sent off her latest partner to fetch her something to drink. Now she sat alone in a quiet nook, enjoying with deep breaths the scents of jasmine and lily that surrounded her. She was a trifle too hot after her exercise and idly waved her fan, eyes closed.

Some sixth sense told her she wasn't alone. "Thank you for . . ." she began. Then she opened her eyes and recoiled slightly. "Oh, it's you."

Sir Niles bowed. "At your service again." He offered her one of the champagne flutes he held.

"Thank you, Sir Niles. But Mr. Dickson has offered to bring me refreshment."

"When his dowager grandmother called him to her side, he delegated the delightful task to me."

She couldn't leave him standing there like a servant proffering a glass. She took it, strangely glad she wore gloves so their fingers did not actually touch. Rose remembered the strange sensation she'd had when he'd taken her hand in Mr. Crenshaw's office.

"You're not wearing your ruby," Sir Niles commented. "I thought you'd be eager to show it off."

"I hope I have better taste than that."

"I hope so too," he said under his breath.

Rose wasn't sure she'd heard him correctly. It wasn't like the punctilious Sir Niles to mutter.

Politeness bade her ask him to sit down. He accepted and sat beside her in silence, also most unlike him. Surely etiquette demanded he make some comment on the weather.

"A charming notion of Lady Fitzmonroe's," she said, doing her duty. She sipped the champagne and managed not to make a face. Accustomed by now to the bubbles and the drying effect on her mouth, she was still striving to get used to the taste.

"All this?" he asked, pushing aside a stray sprig of jasmine that seemed to want to tickle his face. "It seems a lot of effort for something that will fade by tomorrow afternoon."

"But surely any effort is worthwhile if it creates such beauty. It reminds me of the late queen of France's Petite Trianon. Not that I ever saw it. But my father did, a few years before the Revolution."

"So did mine. A pretty piece of make-believe. Lady Fitzmonroe has done very well, considering she hasn't the entire resources of France at her disposal. We might be deep in the middle of the country, no one around for miles."

"Except for the orchestra," Rose reminded him She had never seen Sir Niles in a sportive mood. She wondered if anyone ever had. She also wondered if that was his first glass of champagne. But surely so famed a gamester couldn't be fuddled by any amount of champagne.

"Played by talented sheep, perhaps? Bows held in their little black hooves?"

"And harps plucked by their curly little horns," Rose said, entranced by the image.

"With a dog for conductor."

"Using a shepherd's crook to beat the time!"

Rose smiled into Sir Niles's eyes. But his expression did not match the lightness of his tone. On the contrary, his gaze seemed to burn with an intensity of purpose, in strange contrast to his usual languid manner. Deliberately, he took the cold champagne flute from her hand and put it, together with his, on the floor.

Rose felt a peculiar jumpy sensation in her breast, as though all the champagne bubbles had gathered in one spot and were lifting her heart.

He turned more fully toward her, his hand falling to the seat of the rustic bench they shared. Had he moved it even slightly, he could have touched her knee. She was aware of it as she might be aware of a box of poisoned bonbons. It would be fatally easy to be tempted into doing what would only rebound poorly tomorrow. "Miss Spenser . . . Rose. I wonder if you have ever felt . . ."

Rose opened her eyes wide. "Ever felt . . . what?" she prompted.

But his former cool manner returned. He straightened his back and looked past her ear. Then Rose heard what his quicker senses had already caught.

The sound of feminine laughter, laughter Rose recognized, though with an added flirtatious lilt.

"La, General! How you military men ever have time
for battles!"

With a whisk and whirl of her sheer silk scarf, Aunt
Paige arrived at the bench and slid to a stop, surprise
lifting her eyebrows as she spied her niece. "Rose?"

A large, middle-aged officer, his thinning rust-col-
ored hair out of harmony with his scarlet uniform,
peered at her through slightly protuberant eyes. "This
your little niece, eh? A pleasure." Then he saw Sir
Niles. "Alardyce, isn't it?"

"How do you do, sir?"

"By Saint Pat, it's good to see you again, my boy."
The general let a hint of Irish brogue slip into his otherwise cultured tone. He was shaking Sir Niles's hand
as though assuring himself it was securely attached.

"And you, sir," Sir Niles said, but his voice was swallowed up by the general's emphatic announcement.

"I haven't seen Alardyce since . . . let me see. You
rode up, gave us the order to advance, and rode off.
I made sure you were lost in the next volley."

"Not lost, sir. Temporarily mislaid."

"Eh? Oh, Frenchies got you?"

"Only for half a day, sir. When they were routed,
they left their prisoners behind."

"Ah, yes. In all m'life, I've never seen a prettier sight
than the knapsacks of my enemies, as what's-his-name
said."

"Napoleon, sir?"

"Was it?"

Perhaps feeling it had been long enough since her
swain had noticed her, Aunt Paige rapped his arm
slightly with her fan. "The prettiest sight you've ever
seen? I declare I feel insulted. What about you, Rose?"

"I believe we must make excuses for military men," Rose said, letting her curious eyes rest on Sir Niles. "Living as they do among men alone, they lose the knack for compliments."

"Not entirely," Sir Niles said. "We have our dreams to keep us in practice." He looked at Rose with an ember of his former intensity in his expression. "We must cling to our dreams, no matter how long it takes to achieve them." Taking Aunt Paige's hand in his, he bowed over it. "I shall beat the retreat, Lady Marlton." In his usual unhurried way, he left them.

"I'll find you later, Alardyce," the general said.

"Go now," Aunt Paige said, flicking her fan in his direction. "I know better than to come between a man and his Army acquaintances."

"But, er . . . um." He rolled his eyes toward the bench. "Don't like to leave you alone, m'dear."

"I have my niece to bear me company. You may call on me tomorrow between the hours of eleven and twelve. You will find me quite alone then."

After he'd gone, Aunt Paige sank onto the bench. Rose, laughing a little, joined her. "Who was that extraordinary man?"

"General Sir Augustus O'Banyon, if you please. Quite the most fascinatingly active man. Within ten minutes, he'd routed my most favored friends, danced a gavotte without actually injuring anyone— though one gentleman only saved himself with a leap worthy of a mountain goat—and swept me off to this secluded corner, undoubtedly reconnoitered in advance. It's a lucky chance for me you should have found it already, or heaven knows in what condition I might be at this moment." She sighed ecstatically. "There's really nothing like the army for organization."

"I hadn't realized Sir Niles had been in the army," Rose said slowly.

"He is of the proper age to have served. I shall ask the general about him, if you wish. Tell me, what were you and he speaking of just now? He seemed terribly intent."

"I was . . . we were . . ."

"I trust you weren't warning him of the evils of the way he lives. It's none of your affair; you are too innocent, and heaven forbid you should ever be anything else."

"Isn't it my affair when he embroils my brother in his activities?"

"Alas, no," Aunt Paige said. "Besides, it isn't as though anyone is forcing Rupert into playing so high. Of course, as his aunt, I'm appalled by his extravagance. On the other hand, many men play for great stakes and lose without losing one jot of their consequence. Look at Mr. Brummel."

"Considering, ma'am, that Mr. Brummel was forced, thanks to his debts, into going into exile, I hardly think he is a model for Rupert's behavior."

"But think how long he was the arbiter of all that was fashionable, and one always heard he'd lost prodigious sums. I must say, I wish we could see his like again. Men were so neat then. Now they turn themselves into such figures of fun with their wasp waists and chimney-pot hats."

"Sir Niles always looks like a bandbox figure." Saying his name was the equivalent of prodding a sore tooth to learn if it still hurt.

"Oh, Sir Niles stands alone. Such elegance, such taste, such a restful man. The Countess of Brayle claims he redecorated her drawing room so neatly she never knew workmen were in the house. It was as if the genie of the ring had appeared and arranged the whole matter."

"I didn't know he lent his talents to things other than the design of new cravats and other fripperies."

"Well, the countess is his sister's husband's cousin. Sir Niles only gives his help to relations. I don't believe he cares a flip of his fingers for anyone outside his family. How the man ever hopes to marry . . ."

"Perhaps he doesn't. Not all men marry."

"Oh, I'm confident he's the marrying kind. And of the proper age, now that I think of it. He can't be thirty yet, and that is the age a man starts to plan setting up his nursery."

Aunt Paige sized up her niece with a long slow appraisal that left Rose certain either her hair was coming down or her petticoat was dragging on the floor.

"What is it?" she demanded.

"What were you and he talking of? I couldn't tell because he moved away so quickly, but it almost looked as though I interrupted either an assignation or a proposal. Had you meant to meet him here?"

"Not at all. He brought me champagne, that's all."

"When I saw you last, you were dancing with Mr. Dickson. What became of him?"

"His grandmother wanted him. When I opened my eyes, there stood Sir Niles."

"What were you doing with your eyes closed?"

"I was resting them." They felt like two hot ammunition balls now. "Sir Niles was kind enough to fulfill Mr. Dickson's commission for me. I was very grateful."

At that moment, an incautious movement by Aunt Paige knocked the two forgotten champagne flutes over. One shattered on impact with the gleaming marble floor. The other only fell over, setting up a sweep of echoes as the crystal's ring resonated through the ballroom. It seemed to Rose everyone must come running to see what the commotion was. It must have made less noise that it had seemed to her sitting beside it. The room quickly ceased to chime with echoes.

"My dear Rose," Aunt Paige said, when she'd stopped patting her heart. "I take it Sir Niles laid aside your glasses in this informal manner."

"Yes, he did."

The older woman sighed happily. "In my experience, a man only takes a glass from a woman under two circumstances—both romantic. Either he wants to kiss her or to propose, which in your case comes to the same thing. Tell me at once. Is Sir Niles in love with you?"

Rose thought of the intent, almost hungry, look Sir Niles had turned upon her. Surely that was not the expression of a man on the brink of offering his hand and heart? Yet the burning intensity of his gaze had struck her with more force than any poetic phrase or infatuated compliment ever had.

"I don't think so," she said, weighing her words. "No one would be more surprised than I if he were. Except perhaps Sir Niles himself."

"Whatever do you mean by that?"

"Well, I'm not precisely the sort of girl a man like that marries."

"I hope you are not the sort of girl he doesn't marry, if you follow me."

Rose only shook her head slightly. "I mean, I'm presentable, I hope, but not *dernier cri*. I follow fashion; I don't set it. Nor do I care to. Sir Niles could be happy only, I'm sure, with a woman who lives at the forefront of the mode. Someone very elegant and accomplished. My dearest friends could not call me that."

"You paint very prettily," Aunt Paige said, with the air of one saving one spark of hope from a tidal wave. "And your music has improved very much since Monsieur Quartermain has taken you in hand."

"But I have not a shred of talent, only application. No, the woman Sir Niles marries must be so confident in herself and her abilities that she commands even his respect and admiration. I could never marry a man so far above me in talents. I would diminish and disappear in his shadow."

Aunt Paige brushed her gloved hands together as though disposing of the subject. "Very well. When he proposes, you will turn him down and lose the marriage of the Season." She softened and smiled. "But I wouldn't have you marry any man if you didn't feel he is right for you."

Though she'd made her position as clear as she possibly could to her aunt, Rose found herself pondering Sir Niles's attitude even as she took to the floor again with the charming Colonel Wapton. He was talking pleasantly of the last time they'd met. Rose lent him only part of her attention, nodding and smiling in the right places, when she caught sight of Rupert just entering the ball. His face was so blandly expressionless that Rose knew at once something must be wrong. He wore that look only when in great trouble.

"There's my brother," she said, interrupting the colonel and the dance. "Would you mind very much taking me to him?"

"Certainly not, ma'am. A privilege," he said at once, as she had all but forced him to do.

As they crossed the floor, he mentioned he'd called on her earlier in the day. "I was so sorry to have missed you, Colonel Wapton. Morning callers are always acceptable to my aunt. Oh, except between the hours of eleven o'clock and noon," she added with a mischievous smile.

"I will obey her implicitly, if you'll explain the reason for that charming smile," he said.

"It's nothing, only . . . well, you wouldn't want to discommode a senior officer."

"Who?" the colonel said in a teasing undertone.

"Do you know a General O'Banyon?"

"Only by reputation; we are not in the same regiment. Is he courting your aunt?"

"Shouldn't he?"

"He was notorious with the ladies in Spain. They seemed fascinated by his red hair." He passed his hand over his own undoubtedly ginger-colored hair. "But that won't weigh with Lady Marlton, I hope."

"She seemed charmed, I think." Rose realized such gossip could only harm her aunt, no matter how amusing she found such tales against others. "Here's my brother," she said, poking Rupert in the back. "Rupert, let me present Colonel Wapton. Colonel Wapton, my brother, Rupert Spenser."

The two men bowed. Then Rupert's eye lighted upon the colonel's dark green uniform facings. "I say, weren't the lot of you at Salamanca?"

"Yes, we were. Not me, though. I was laid up in the hospital with a broken thigh."

Rupert's momentary animation drained away, leaving the signs of his misery plain even to a stranger's eyes. "Care for some punch, Rose?" he asked. "Know you don't like champagne." He drained his glass of the delicate straw-colored wine. "Dashed thin stuff."

"Thank you; I should love some punch."

The colonel stayed by her side while Rupert stalked away. "Army mad, I perceive?"

"Since infancy. My late uncle made the mistake of sending him a toy rifle and real forage cap when Rupert was only six or seven. I remember how he'd pore over every newspaper my father received, desperately following the news of every battle. He's been wild to join . . . ah, well."

"He should buy his commission. He's the sort we need in the army now that the war is at an end. Someone who loves the service, not just the profits to be made from it."

"Someone like you, Colonel?" Rose asked gently.

Colonel Wapton colored and cleared his throat. "Not at all. I'm an opportunist. I care for nothing but my pay and my perquisites."

"Seriously . . ."

"We are at a ball, Miss Spenser. Being serious is against the law. But come, tell me why your brother isn't in uniform at this moment, hotheaded youngster that he is."

"There speaks the voice of a man who is what—thirty?"

"You flatter me," he said, bowing. Rose had been, just a little. "I received my present rank at the age of thirty-five. I'm now not quite forty."

"A sensible age."

"Not too sensible," he admitted with a flirtatious gleam in his amber eyes. Rose only waved her fan and smiled. "Is there some physical reason for your brother's remaining a civilian?"

"Yes, very definitely. My father."

"I don't follow."

"My father is adamantly against Rupert serving in any capacity in the army, navy, or horse marines. He is terrified Rupert will be killed. He had a younger brother, you see, who died a very few months after

taking his commission. My father recalls very clearly
that Uncle Rupert was as excited as a schoolboy over
putting on his uniform."

"And having named his son for his brother, he is
afraid the same fate will befall the boy. Superstitious,
but intelligible."

"Unfortunately, Rupert can't see it that way." Rose
caught herself. She shouldn't be so frank with a
stranger. "Forgive me for rattling on so, Colonel. I'm
sure you wish to be amusing yourself."

"I can think of nothing I wish to do just now, Miss
Spenser, except to offer you whatever help lies in my
power should your brother choose to take up the service upon his majority. He's almost old enough now,
isn't he?"

"Yes, he is. And thank you for your kind offer, but
until my father relents, Rupert will not act against his
wishes."

"Every word you say convinces me more that he's
good officer material. But I can see you wish to talk to
him alone, so I'll leave you with him." He bowed to
Rose, smartly including Rupert with a click of his
heels.

Rupert handed Rose a glass of pink punch, and she
lost her sense of being in the ballroom as she recalled
Sir Niles's taking her glass away. Had his fingers trem-
bled the merest bit as he touched her hand? Drat her
gloves! Now she couldn't be certain.

As though a flame passed over her skin, Rose suddenly found herself breathless and shaken and much,
much too warm. What if Sir Niles could have fallen in
love with her? Wouldn't she then be forced to ask herself whether she really despised him or whether there
were some deeper feelings at work?

But no, she bore no such tender emotions in her

breast for him. She was certain of it. Farthest thing from her mind. No question.

She drew a long, slow breath. There. All was well. Whatever strange excitement she felt was merely natural female triumph at the prospect of having the great Sir Niles a humble supplicant at her feet for all the fashionable world to see.

"Who was that jackanapes?" Rupert asked irritably.

"Who? Oh, Colonel Wapton. A very amusing gentleman."

"Is he? Lucky dog, anyway. He has the chance of getting out of this damned hothouse."

"You don't care for Lady Fitzmonroe's ideas?" Rose said, feeling her heart sink. She recognized Rupert's mood as one of reckless despair fueled by too much alcohol.

"What?" He glanced around, and she realized he hadn't even noticed the profusion of flowers. "I meant society. The *ton*. All that rot."

His voice had risen. Rose laid her hand on his arm. "I'm tired, Rupert. Would you take me home?"

"What about Aunt Paige? I should do my duty by her."

"She's having much too good a time flirting with generals to mind either of us."

"Eh? She dashed well should mind you. You're in her charge, and I don't like finding you with coxcomb officers, wandering about on your own."

"Such heat," she said, laughing artificially and turning him aside with such adroitness that he found himself taking her arm rather than reaching for another glass of wine. "We cannot criticize our good aunt. She enjoys her life, and after two husbands she has the right."

Chattering lightly, she escorted her brother to the

door, accepted her cloak, and saw him into their carriage. The last person she saw as the footman closed the door was Sir Niles Alardyce leaving the house. He did not look in her direction.

Five

"How much?" Rose sat frozen against the cushions as their carriage rolled over the cobbles.

Rupert told her the figure again. He seemed to be smiling, as if pleased by her reaction. It was as if he had lost a thousand pounds only to give her a delightful surprise.

"That's in total," Rose said hopefully.

"No. That's tonight."

Her voice gone to nothing but a squeaky thread, Rose tried twice to speak before achieving sound. "Tonight? You lost a thou-thousand pounds tonight? But all your IOUs . . . Sir Niles must hold . . ."

"Another thousand, perhaps. Most other fellows hold notes for two or three hundred each."

"Each?"

"About that."

All thought of romance or happiness disappeared, crushed under the weight of this news. "What is your total of indebtedness, Rupert? Do you know the full figure?"

"Of course," he snapped. "Or at least, I would if I thought about it for a bit."

Her head throbbed in time to the horses' clattering hooves. "Two or three thousand no doubt."

"Something on that order, yes. But I won't go to Father so don't trouble yourself on that score. Not after the things he said to me last year."

She had not been present on that occasion. Not that she'd needed to be. Her father's voice had a peculiar carrying quality left over from the days when he'd studied for the clergy, and whatever she'd not heard then, Rupert had told her later. The interview had been shattering for both parties. Rupert had threatened to run away, and her father had been so white and sweating that her mother had sent for the apothecary.

"What will you do?" Rose asked.

He shrugged pettishly. "Recovering the smaller chits isn't a difficulty. Most of them are good fellows and won't mind waiting for quarter-day, though I shall be on deuced short commons after I pay 'em. They've all been in the same condition one time or another, and I've let them run on tick 'til their allowances come due."

"Then there's no difficulty," Rose said, sighing with relief.

"Not with my special friends, no. But there's Crawford. He's a cash-down man who wasn't happy to take paper anyway. He'll cut up stiff if I don't pay him first."

"Then pay him. I'll gladly give you what I have left from my pin money."

He looked a trifle hangdog at that, but didn't refuse her offer. "You're the best sister a fellow could have. I only wish that ruby had been worthy of a queen. Then I would have figured it came to the correct hand."

"Save your compliments for those who want them," Rose said, mimicking their nursery maid, the only female in three counties not charmed by Rupert from his cradle.

He laughed shortly, but the worry lines didn't fade from his forehead. They disturbed Rose, for they made her younger brother look old before his time. Old and dissolute, like the men who congregated in the card rooms at parties, their faces still painted in the style of thirty years ago to cover the ravages of debauchery and disease.

Perhaps it was just the flicker of the widely spaced lamps that gave him that unhealthy look, but Rose didn't like it. She vowed privately to write to her mother tonight, pleading with her to use her influence to get their father to relent. It was this kicking of heels when he longed to be up and doing that caused Rupert to waste his time and his substance at the gaming hells of London.

"What's truly troubling you?" she asked softly.

"It's the paper Alardyce holds. Besides tonight's thousand, I owe him at least another five hundred. It's a wonder he hasn't come dunning me yet, though everyone knows he's rich beyond telling. What good's my measly fifteen hundred to him? Why can't he just tear up the papers? It's nothing to him, and it's life or death to me." He paused and seemed to sober, though tears dripped from his cheeks. "Life or death," he repeated, staring out the window at the chill night.

Rose gripped his arm tightly through the thinness of his sleeve. She could feel the strength of his forearm muscles, honed by years of neck-or-nothing riding, wasted now on holding cards or squiring fat matrons through dances. "There must be a way. Perhaps if I went to him . . ."

"No," he said, jerking his arm free. "It's a debt of honor. I either pay it or blow out my brains. There's no other path."

Chilled, Rose tried to calm him. "Don't be hasty," she said. "Just . . . don't be hasty."

Seeing him into his valet's hands, Rose let her maid undress her and help her into an undyed cashmere dressing gown before dismissing her to brush out her gown. She sat down at her vanity and drew forward a little pot of ink. The letter to her mother took only a few minutes. After sealing it, she took another piece of paper, then sat there biting the end of the feather until the ink dried on the tip.

"Well," she said aloud, "the beginning is easy enough."

Dear Sir Niles, she wrote in a small, sloping hand. Then the ink dried again as she tried to write plainly, yet without giving anything away, and neatly. *Do please join me at Lady Marlton's house between the hours of eleven and noon tomorrow. I shall be quite alone. I wish to discuss matters of a serious nature regarding your activities on this evening and previous evenings. Yours faithfully, Rose Spenser.*

She studied it critically, finding it cold, businesslike, and clear. If it were true, as Aunt Paige suspected, that he had deeper and warmer feelings for her, he'd come merely to see her again. If not, he'd come out of curiosity—or so Rose hoped.

Once the letter was sealed, she rang for her maid and gave instructions that the letter was to be delivered as soon as someone could be found to carry it. Giggling, Lucy promised to hand it to the footman herself, obviously thinking my lady's country cousin had a love affair on hand.

Sighing, Rose climbed into bed at last. Now she had only to sleep and to wait. But sleep came hard, for over and over she experimented with what she would say. Everything depended on his mood. If he had retreated again behind his mask of irony and indifference, she would not be balked, but she would find her task so much more difficult than if he were still gentle as he'd been tonight. She fell asleep thinking of him.

"Sir Niles," Mr. Beringer said jovially, opening the door himself. "I'm so happy you decided to call on me."

"You've hardly left me any choice."

"Come. Don't be like that. We have a mutual interest, and you must consider me a friend."

"A friend? Hardly. I choose my friends with care."

"I can't blame you for being hostile. So many people have difficulty seeing on which side their bread is buttered at first. But only at first. Soon you'll see what a good friend I can be."

Like a sheepdog running circles round a belligerent ram, Mr. Beringer escorted Sir Niles into his well-appointed library.

"You live very well," Sir Niles grudgingly admitted, admiring despite himself the faux paneling and rows of leather-bound books. The red and blue carpet under his feet had the gleam of real silk, while the few candles that lit this splendor were of the finest, whitest wax. The fire that roared in the stone fireplace was perhaps too much for so late in the year, but it gave forth the scent of applewood to perfume the air.

"That is praise indeed, for I know your reputation as a man of taste. A little brandy?"

"Thank you."

"There, you see. We shall be very good friends ere long."

Sir Niles made no answer, but seated himself, his posture easy. Beringer gave him his snifter and took one himself behind the massively carved desk at one end of the room. He adjusted a candle stand with reflector that stood at his elbow to cast more light onto Sir Niles than onto himself.

"Is it to your liking?" he asked, like any eager-to-please host.

"Excellent. Better than what they serve at my club."

"Again you honor me." His chuckles spread outward, setting his great stomach to shaking. If one stuck an olive on a toothpick into the point of a turnip and then gave the turnip thin legs, the result would be very like Mr. Beringer. He obviously enjoyed the finer things of life, for in addition to his elegant home, his clothes were quite well made, considering the technical difficulties involved in clothing a turnip.

Niles drained the glass, grateful for the warmth it created. He'd walked from Lady Fitzmonroe's, hoping the air would drive Rose from his head. He saw she could easily make a fool of him, bringing him to break his resolutions, now on the point of their completion. He had not thought himself so weak when it came to temptation, but seeing her there alone, he'd been unable to resist talking to her. It would have been pleasant to kiss her, but her aunt's timely arrival had prevented it.

Just as well. One did not kiss girls of Rose Spenser's respectability unless marriage was in one's mind. And nothing could be farther from his thoughts, no matter what his attorney thought.

"Enough of compliments," he said. "Let's to business."

"Good." Beringer finished his wine as well. "As I indicated in my note, certain facts have come to my attention. Facts which, as a friend, I am happy to hold my tongue about."

"I accept."

Beringer held up his hand. "I like all my clients to know a few things before they accept my friendship."

"All your clients?"

The heavyset man looked a trifle embarrassed. "Many people have secrets, Sir Niles. No one is perfect. Frequently, as with yourself, these are secrets better kept from society's ears."

"And so you keep the proof secure."

"Precisely."

"For a price."

He spread wide his hands. "What would you? A man must live, and I, unfortunately, did not receive those gifts which enable me to live as I please. I like to live well, as you can see."

"I am yearning to know what part you envision for me in your life of leisure."

"A few hundred a year. You won't even miss it. Surely keeping your secret is worth that. Imagine what you would lose if it became known your dearest friend and closest relation died so ignominiously and under such a black cloud."

"True. Very well. I shall send you a check in the morning."

"Excellent. Now, as to the rest of my . . . reward?"

"What else?" Niles sank down again in his chair.

"Among intimate friends, many secrets are exchanged. Perhaps you know some things I should also know. For instance, why Felicia Sanderling had to retire so suddenly from the Season last year. Dale Sanderling is one of your friends, I believe. And the question of the Countess of Danforth's pearls has long been exercising my mind. Does her husband know they were exchanged for fakes?"

"I don't know those things, and if I did, I shouldn't

tell you. I wouldn't deliver my friends to your blood-sucking ways."

Beringer didn't flush or show any sensitivity to the insult. He simply went on in the most natural style. "But that is part of the price. Didn't you understand me? Two secrets a year and five hundred pounds. Then no one need know of Christian's little fault."

"Who told you of it?"

"Of what?"

"'Christian's little fault.' Which of my friends is already in your clutches, Beringer?"

"I don't wish to create ill feeling, so I shan't tell you. Rest assured, however, that your secret is safe with me."

Niles knew no one except Crenshaw knew the facts in Christian's case, Crenshaw and the three men who had betrayed him to his doom. He studied Beringer. The once trim officer had run to fat with his civilian ways. Yet Niles didn't underestimate his opponent. He still retained enough strength and speed to make a stand-up fight a very chancy business. His gray eyes were never still, flicking over Niles, anticipating any move toward violence.

"Very well," Niles said, sighing and sitting back as though he'd become boneless. "I'll find out the answers."

"Are you certain you don't know them already?"

"You'll want proof, I'm sure."

"Always acceptable. Documentary evidence is so hard to argue against."

"You haven't shown me any evidence."

"It is here." From under the blotter, Beringer pulled out a thin dossier. "All the facts—dates, times, accusations, affidavits. Sworn to by his two dearest friends, who could have no reason to lie." Beringer slid a paper into Niles's hand.

"Roland Curtman . . ." Niles mused. "Is that the same Curtman who was so recently brought down by the Black Mask?"

For the first time, Beringer seemed ill at ease. He twitched all over, almost shuddering. "A foolish man. Greed, it seems, was ever his downfall. I warned him."

"You had 'befriended' him, too?"

"The Black Mask wasn't the first to look at Curtman's secret records. Alas, a profitable friendship in many ways now severed. It makes me all the more delighted to bring you into the circle of my friends."

"You leave me no choice but to join that company. But I shall want to see the proof of which you speak."

"Naturally. I would expect nothing less from a man of your intelligence." Beringer picked up the dossier on his desk, then, with deliberation, put it down again. "I must insist, with the greatest delicacy, of course, that you give me your word you won't attempt to destroy these. I obtained them only with considerable expense. Their destruction would require me and thus, you, to be put to that expense again."

"You have my word." Sir Niles held out his hand imperiously.

"The whole painful story, eh, Sir Niles?" Beringer said, after watching the younger man read in silence.

"Yes, as you say." With a cavalier gesture, he tossed the file back onto the desk. "Will you accept my check?"

Beringer patted the air soothingly. "With the greatest reluctance to give offense, Sir Niles, I will not. An enterprise like mine requires cash down."

"Very well. I shall send it by messenger in the morning."

"And as for the rest?"

"I will reflect upon those secrets I know and choose among them for your delectation."

"Choose carefully, for both our sakes."

The tall-case clock standing against the wall dropped eleven mellifluous notes into the conversation. Beringer peered at the clock face. "I'm pleased we have come to so easy an understanding, Sir Niles. The interest I have found in your conversation has tempted me into forgetting the lateness of the hour. May I see you out?"

"Certainly." Sir Niles rose after Beringer and let the older man usher him to the door. "I must confess I appreciate your attitude. So many men in your position would have blustered and threatened. You set out your terms so politely . . . well, I needn't tell you what great store I set by civility."

"Ah, you are justly famed for your manners, Sir Niles. It is a genuine pleasure to deal with you. Not all of my friends are so delightful. The one I await now . . . but I am indiscreet. A grievous error for one in my profession."

"I quite understand. You'll forgive me if I don't shake your hand."

"Quite. Good evening, Sir Niles."

After Sir Niles was gone, Beringer hesitated, glancing toward his library. He could just glimpse the corner of his desk, knowing Sir Niles's dossier rested on the blotter. Prudence dictated he return and put it away at once. On the other hand, as a man of full body and indolent nature, he was reluctant to put himself to any extra physical effort. In a moment, his next appointment would appear. Better to wait here ready to open the door.

Within five minutes, he bowed deeply, greeting the elderly lady on the threshold. "Save your imitations of the manners of better men," she said in a cracked contralto. "Let's get to business."

"As you wish, your grace. Come into the library, where it is warmer."

Stepping ahead of him, she threw back her veil to reveal features once famous more for liveliness than beauty, yet fascinating enough to snare one of the great lords of the country for her husband. Though elderly now, her carriage remained effortless, and her dark eyes had no less snap and ginger than when she had been a girl.

She glanced at the brandy glasses still on the desk. "Entertaining plenty of company, aren't you? How do I know we're alone?"

"You have my word, your grace."

"Hmmph. Save your breath."

"Very well," Beringer said silkily, knowing he had the upper hand. "You are at liberty to search."

"I don't care to spend another minute with scum like you. You claim to have uncovered a disreputable secret about my daughter. Let's have it."

From beneath his desk blotter, Beringer drew forth a second dossier. "On or about the fifteenth of September, eighteen-ought-five, her ladyship was brought to bed of a boy, presently known as Robert, Marquis of . . ."

"Tell me something I don't know," the duchess said, though a close observer would have seen her cheeks grow pale under her brave paint.

Mr. Beringer prided himself on his observational skills. "Very well. In late January of that same year, her ladyship was visiting Parmeter House with a party of friends. Her husband was not with her. I have here statements from the chambermaid, a valet, and an undermaid that on at least three mornings, her ladyship was not alone in her bed. The inference must therefore be drawn, with the aid of a little elementary mathematics . . ."

"Enough! You're a long-winded devil. Instead of gouging your betters, you should stand for Parliament."

"Too much work for me, your grace. I am a man of simple pleasures. Good food, good wine, the leisure to digest properly, these are my joys."

"How much do you want?" she said, cutting to the point.

He told her. She refused absolutely to give him any information regarding her friends, but, after a word picture of the ruination of her daughter's marriage and her grandson's future, relented to the extent of offering to exchange political secrets she was privy to as the wife of a leading politician.

"Very well," she said finally. "How shall I pay you? I haven't any money of my own."

"I am aware of it, your grace. However, I believe you possess a certain necklace that never leaves your skin? Aphrodite's Tears?"

"My . . . my necklace?" For the first time in the interview, the duchess seemed shaken, her hand seeking the high collar of her velvet dress. Beringer noticed she was staring past his shoulder.

"Very well." With a grand gesture, she jerked the piece from her throat and threw it, jangling, at Beringer's feet.

Though stout, Beringer was willing to bend for such a prize. The necklace, a dazzle of baroque pink pearls and diamonds, swung from his hand. A genuine smile lit Beringer's face. "Truly a treasure beyond price."

"You can never sell it," the duchess charged. "It's too famous."

"Sell it? Never. No, nor break it up, either. I shall keep it safe . . . yes, safe."

"You'd better take care," the duchess said. "I have

been warned the Black Mask has an interest in such things."

"The Black Mask?" Beringer repeated. "Why threaten me with that bugaboo?"

"Curtman didn't find him so."

"Curtman again? Curtman was a fool and always has been. Even as a young man, he never showed any flair, such as is my genius."

"You knew him?"

"Of course. A useful tool at times, but it was always I who thought of our schemes. Our other friend showed more courage, but he was weakened by the restraints of conscience."

"Other friend?" The duchess's voice seemed deeper.

"I am being indiscreet . . ." Beringer said. "I shall stop."

"I hope you enjoy your comeuppance when it arrives," she said bitterly.

"I? I'm as safe as houses, your grace. Who could prosecute me without exposing themselves? I have all the evidence hidden away. If the authorities come and dare to search, they won't find anything I don't wish them to find. Think of the embarrassment to yourself and your family. Our business is concluded, your grace. I bid you a good evening."

He turned aside, holding up the necklace so that the pearls gleamed like sunset-colored moons in the candlelight and the diamonds offered their frigid beauty. He wasn't even aware of the duchess' departure, his courtesy and caution failing.

After gloating a few minutes, he remembered with visible alarm that he'd not yet hidden away the two dossiers on his desk. Dangerous if the duchess came back with friends or, worse yet, a magistrate. He liked the location of his home, but knew there were several magistrates living within a few minutes' walk. If the duchess appeared on one of their doorsteps, they would listen to her. And his strongbox was not easy of access on purpose. It took time to reach it.

On the other side of the room, the bookcases rose to the ceiling. A rolling ladder made it possible to obtain those books otherwise out of easy reach.

With the dossiers under one arm and the necklace still dangling from his hand, Beringer tottered and huffed his way up. At the top, he paused, breathing heavily.

Then he pushed aside one section of the bookcase, revealing that the books were no more than spines and an inch of cover, glued to a flat panel. So long as no one tried to pull out a copy of one of the very dull books—mostly sermons—the illusion was perfect. Behind the panel was his strongbox, locked with a cunning pressure lock. It took just the right touch to open and even he, with all his practice, sometimes was driven to the swearing point before it opened.

The dossiers slipped from beneath his arm and fluttered down like wounded birds. As he glanced down, saying, "Damnation!" by a lucky chance his hand pushed forward in such a way as to open the lock. With a heavy sigh, stuffing the necklace into his pocket, Beringer started down the ladder to collect the papers blowing about the carpet.

Two steps from the bottom, he paused, doubting. Where had the draft come from? His beautifully paneled library was never drafty. He hated drafts, blowing cold down the back of his neck when all he wanted was quiet, warmth, and comfort. Now a significant draft was making the candle flames dance. Beringer looked around wildly, the chill on his skin sinking down to his bones when he saw the figure standing silently by the curtains.

"You!"

"I." The slim figure, clad all in black even to the inky leather mask that clung to his white cheeks and brow, walked slowly forward. He held his voice to a harsh whisper.

"What do you want?"

"Come, come. Let us not play such foolish games, Beringer. You know why I have come. The same reason I appeared to Curtman. His evil ways drew me to him. They say, don't they, that the devil claims his own?"

Six

"Do you claim to be some diabolical angel of vengeance? You're nothing but a common thief!"

"And you are an uncommon one . . . no!"

Beringer cast one desperate glance upward and tried in a mad scramble to reach his secret cache. But the whip-like figure of the Black Mask flashed across the room, seized the heavier man by the tails of his coat, and yanked. Beringer tumbled off the ladder, striving to stay upright. But his heel slipped on one of the loose pages, and he fell with a crash that shook some of the genuine books off the shelves.

A silver-mounted pistol appeared in the mountebank's hand. "Don't move."

With a great deal more elegance than Beringer displayed, the Black Mask whisked up the ladder to peer into the secret horde. Even though his attention seemed to be on what he saw, the pistol never wavered in its aim over Beringer's heart. No sooner had Beringer stolen out a fat hand to give the ladder a push that would shake the interloper off than the finger on the trigger tightened.

"I really shouldn't, if I were you," the Black Mask said. "It would be such a pleasure to kill you."

With a sweeping of his arm, the Black Mask sent everything tumbling down over Beringer's quivering form. Papers, small boxes, miniature paintings cascaded in a seemingly never-ending fall, Beringer flinching under it all.

The dark figure stepped down from the ladder after being certain the box was empty. "My, my, such an extensive collection. Whatever shall we do with so much? I know . . ." He pointed a commanding finger toward the fireplace.

"No. You don't understand. You have no idea how much I've paid . . . listen, there's plenty for us both. We'll be partners," Beringer said, sweating. "You can't expect to go on robbing forever. You'll end on the gallows. Be sensible. You can't ask me to burn my life's work."

"You'll make me weep in a minute."

"Look. Look at this." The fat man scooped up a box and flipped open the latch. A brilliant cascade of rainbows seemed to float in the air. "They give me their jewels when they have no money. Look. A fortune. Diamonds, emeralds, sapphires. All yours, if you go away and leave me in peace."

"These papers must be burnt."

"No, I beg of you."

"Yes. Come now. You need the exercise. I fear you lead an unhealthy life." The comment was punctuated with a wave of the pistol.

Trip after weary trip, in fear of his life, the blackmailer carried all his hardwon spoils to the inferno. He cowered back from the intense heat as indiscretions, infatuations, and immoralities burned. Paper, blackened to floating ash, flew up the chimney.

While Beringer labored, the Black Mask stirred the rubbish with his booted foot, kicking aside the assorted jewel boxes that lay, like fat oysters pregnant with pearls, among the papers. "How do your victims explain the loss of so many pretties to their fathers and husbands?"

"I don't know," Beringer snapped, his face dirty and sweating. "I don't concern myself with their problems."

A certain crest caught the quick-moving eyes behind the mask. Quickly, he scooped up the case. Flipping it open, he saw the miniature of a sweet-faced girl, hardly sixteen, with round eyes and a soft mouth, done in ivory with diamonds around the frame. "Bella Fortescue."

"It's not my fault the silly wench drowned herself," Beringer said sulkily. "I told her no one would find out if she kept her gob shut. S'not as if she were pregnant. I told her no one would know she wasn't a virgin if she didn't tell 'em."

"But she was in love with William Perry and couldn't face him."

"Silly wench. She could have got her hands on the Perry fortune. Enough for all of us in those pockets. But she had to go drown herself in the Serpentine. Fat lot of good that money does me in the grave."

"You are unspeakably vile, sir." It was so much his own thought that for an instant, Niles thought he'd spoken aloud. Then he saw the duchess in the doorway. He scowled. He had been embarrassed almost beyond bearing when he'd returned in his persona of the Black Mask to confront Beringer, having confirmed as Sir Niles that Beringer was indeed the blackmailer who, rumor whispered, had long preyed upon society. For some reason, probably his own sense of the romantic, he'd expected Beringer's next "client" to be some young woman in trouble. But to come back and find a woman, well known not only to the world but to his own family, had been almost

enough to make him save Beringer's exposure for another evening.

She entered with the same confident bearing she'd
shown earlier. "Good evening, Black Mask. I've heard
of you."

He bowed, afraid his voice would give him away.

Looking toward the fireplace, she sniffed. "A grand
auto-da-fé of the evidence, I see. No matter. Perhaps
it's just as well."

"Your own are burnt as well," Niles said hoarsely.

"Excellent. If you hadn't, I should have had to."

"Is that why you came back?"

"No. Magistrate Howe is rousing his minions and
has promised to meet me here."

"He won't find anything," Beringer exulted. "That
one is too clever for his own good. There's no more
evidence."

"I believe my unsupported word should be enough.
If I, with my name, stand in the dock and proclaim
that you attempted to extort money from me by
threats of exposure, you'll be lucky to be transported.
They might even hang you."

Beringer's cheeks were pale as uncooked pork,
but he tried to bluster. "You wouldn't dare! You'd
be ruined."

The duchess gave the ringing laugh that had, more
than anything else, made her the toast of London in
her day. "Ruined? I? I have been ruined and re-
deemed a dozen times. Didn't you ever hear how I
was abducted at nineteen and not returned for a
week? Or that my second girl bears far too clear a resemblance to a certain cardinal now living in Rome?"

Beringer's eyes were avid even through his fear, obviously plotting how to use this information given so
freely. "You don't dare expose yourself."

The duchess looked at him dispassionately. "I am very old, Mr. Beringer. They can't hurt me now. As long as my daughter and grandson are safe, I don't care what anyone says about me. They've said it before. You, however, should care."

"What's to stop me telling the world about your precious grandson? If I'm ruined, he'll go down too!"

Niles took the man by the lapel and shook him as a cook shakes a jellybag. "Speak civil, rot you, or you'll never live to stand that trial."

Behind him, the duchess spoke softly. "Tell about my grandson and you'll stand convicted out of your own mouth. The jury won't even leave the box. And then you'll hang by your bull-like throat until you are dead. I've seen dozens of hangings. Fat men seldom break their necks. Their friends come and pull on their legs until they die. Have you any friends, Mr. Beringer?"

Beringer subsided into a moaning lump.

Ignoring him, the duchess touched Niles on the arm. "You'd better be off. Magistrates are not imaginative men."

"Dunno what you mean."

"I mean twice now you have discovered rather obscure men to be nothing less than criminals. Once might be accidental; twice begins to look like good staff work. I think if I had a guilty conscience, I would start locking my windows more carefully. Not to mention concealing any incriminating evidence beyond the cunning of mere man."

"Dunno what you mean."

"Of course not. Nevertheless, you have done me and mine a good turn this evening. I should hate to see your gallant career end on the scaffold next to that miserable object. So take this plunder and be gone."

Niles looked down at the piles of jewelry boxes. "Will you take charge of it all? See it returns to its owners."

"You don't want it?"

Niles shook his head. "Being a lady, you can give 'em their baubles back and not a soul the wiser. Maybe there's some wives who'd like to have their old necklaces back without their husbands knowing. Me, I'd have t'drop 'em off in the post, and they're a disreputable lot."

Some dismay shown on the duchess's face. "I shall need a satchel to transport it all, but I accept your commission on the understanding that you leave at once. It's not at all safe."

"I don't like to leave you with him," he said, flicking one finger toward Beringer. The man quivered as though under a lash.

"Never mind about him." With a little difficulty, for the hammer kept tangling in the lace, the duchess pulled a small pistol from her dainty reticule. "I don't like to shoot things, but I assure you I am quite capable of doing so."

Niles escaped out the window just as the rattle of heavy boots came over the threshold. He cocked an ear and grinned when he heard the duchess say, "You certainly took your time about it. I've had time to stand off him and a dozen like him."

Half an hour later, Sir Niles Alardyce, a little less neat than usual, left the stable mews shared by the dozen or so young men of fashion who dwelt in the square. To all appearances, he'd either been saying good night to his horses or arranging the use of them in the morning.

When he entered his chambers on the second floor, he all but tripped over his man, asleep in a chair. "Letter for you, Sir Niles," he said, sitting up suddenly and blinking owlishly at the candle his master held.

"Letter? You're dreaming, Baxter. Go to bed."

"Never on duty, Sir Niles." He shifted in the armchair and pulled a white square of paper from between the cushions. "Here, sir. All present and correct. The bloke what delivered it intimated there was a lady waiting on pins and needles for an answer."

Though permitted considerable freedom of expression by his master, Baxter knew a sore point when came to Sir Niles's reputation with the females. Unlike the other gentlemen's gentlemen's masters, Sir Niles never confided either triumphs or disappointments to his valet's sympathetic ear. Frequently, he knew only of the beginning or termination of an amour when told the particulars by one of his colleagues. This naturally injured Baxter's pride.

By the judicious offer of beer, he'd solicited the name of the lady who had sent the letter. But Miss Rose Spenser didn't sound the sort of female Sir Niles usually chose for an inamorata. No, Baxter didn't care for what he heard from the footman. Miss Rose Spenser sounded like the sort of girl a man like Sir Niles married, and Baxter liked holding bachelor household. "Women," he frequently averred while lifting a pint, "women get *into* things."

"Very well, Baxter," Sir Niles said, reading the script. "Get to bed, man. I'm rising at six to ride with Buzzy Harbottle in the Park."

He read the note with close attention, weighing each word. What could she know of his activities as the Black Mask? Nothing. He dismissed the idea she'd somehow divined his secret. He read the note again. No. Whatever she wanted to discuss, it wasn't that.

Later, sitting by the window, he moved the window curtain aside. He didn't know which was Rose's window. For all he knew, her bedroom was at the front of Lady Marlton's house and didn't overlook their gardens at all. Yet often, especially late at night, he would look toward the other house, wondering if Rose were also sleepless.

Niles pondered whether he should call on Rose as she asked or if it would be safer to send some excuse. Something about her made him want to do foolish things, an unneeded distraction at this time in his life when he was so close to completing his vengeance.

When he'd come upon her in Lady Fitzmonroe's unreal garden, sitting there with her eyes closed like a goddess awaiting her worshippers, it had been like a dream. And, as in a dream, he was free to do what he most wanted to do. Fortunately, they'd been interrupted before he could commit any foolish act.

Niles found it difficult to analyze why Rose Spenser, of all women, had this effect on him. True, she was lovely. Her clear, porcelain skin, brightened by pink cheeks, was set off by rich curling hair, almost coffee-colored. Yet beauty alone had never interested him. As much as her appearance, her candor charmed him. Her sweetly serious eyes looked at him so straightforwardly. Too many girls simpered and were either naturally shy or told to be so by their mamas. But Rose looked right at him and did not approve, it seemed, of what she saw. That had pleased his taste.

At the same time, however, he had to admit she seemed to lack fire. She disapproved, but coldly. Just as well, perhaps. If Rose possessed honesty, beauty, *and* passion, he would be doomed to love her. As matters stood, however, he flattered himself he was safe. She came nearer to being his ideal than any woman he'd ever met, but he would not settle for only part of his dreams.

Niles fell to thinking of the raid on Beringer's house and of his near apoplexy when the duchess walked in. By a lucky chance, what had seemed an unexpected complication turned out to be an asset. He had always intended to deprive Beringer of his foul livelihood, but had been reluctant to expose him publicly. To do so would cause all sorts of revelations. Nile had no wish to ruin people. That meant, of course, that Beringer would be free to collect again all his interesting facts. But if the duchess really would prosecute him . . . Sir Niles, for one, would not desert her. Nor, if his influence had any value, would the *ton*. Old scandals didn't, as a rule, interest people much, he knew. There were all too many fresh ones to be discussed.

In the morning, Niles rode with Buzzy Harbottle, usually a reliable lightning rod for any gossip going. "I say," Harbottle said in greeting, "I've had a very bright thought. Dashed if I wasn't awake half the night thinking it over."

"Don't keep me in suspense, old boy," Niles said, mounting his restless horse. The gelding tried to fight him. Niles turned him in a tight circle, getting him under control.

"That beast of yours will have you off in a minute."

"Not him," Niles said, patting the proud bay neck. "He's just eager for a canter."

"Don't know why you keep a creature like that in London. He's more suited to the High Toby than a respectable gentleman's mount."

"Don't you know? When the play goes against me, I take to highway robbery. A man needs a fleet horse under him when the bullets are flying past his ears."

Buzzy looked at him with some doubt. Then he grinned. "I never know your mood, Alardyce. Sometimes I would take my oath you are not joking."

Niles let that pass. "What's your bright thought?"

"Eh? Oh. It's this. Occurred to me at midnight. Best hour of the day for thinking, that is, 'specially if you've had a drink or two."

"And what jewel of thought did your binge bring forth?" Niles asked, amused, as the silence stretched. The wide streets were quiet except for a few early morning riders and a few late-to-bed revelers still in evening dress. It was actually possible to hear a bird sing in one of the pocket-sized parks they passed.

"Well," Buzzy said diffidently. "You know m'sister's holding this masquerade next week. Don't approve of 'em as a rule; too likely to turn into orgies."

"Orgies? I must attend more of your sister's parties."

"Don't mean that," Buzzy said with a blush. "But romping, kiss-in-a-corner, torn laces. That sort of thing."

"Buzzy, I never knew you were a poet."

The inarticulate peer blushed harder but persevered. "Not the thing, and so I told her. But she's got a maggot in her head that she's to outdo Lady Fitzmonroe. Frankly, all the ladies are half mad with jealousy after last night."

"It was a remarkable exhibition. I hate to think what it must have cost."

"Oh, Fitzmonroe's pockets are deep enough to stand the nonsense. Wish I had half his income."

"Hard up?"

"Damnably. That's the other benefit of my idea. Won't cost a thing 'cept for the loo mask. I imagine one's man can dye a pair of old Inexpressibles black."

Niles caught a hint of Buzzy's bright idea and started to grin. "You aren't planning to attend dressed as the Black Mask, Buzzy?"

"Why not?" Buzzy said defensively. "Ain't all the girls mad about him? More than ever after the other day. I think I'd make quite a hit."

"Yes, you would. You and the twelve other geniuses who are likely to think of the same disguise."

"You don't think there'd be that many, do you?"

"Cheer up. The more of you who dress alike, the more fun you'll have. No girl will know which man kissed her."

That reminded him of Rose and a kiss not taken. He stared forward, between his horse's ears. "What day is your sister's party?"

"Wednesday next. Do you want an invitation?"

"Would she have me?"

"My dear fellow, she'll jump at the chance. Ain't your usual thing, though. Company won't be what you like."

"I hope I don't hold myself above whatever company I find myself in."

"No, 'course not. You're not high in the instep, and so I'll tell m'sister."

Niles rode on, controlling his horse automatically with knees and hands. A half smile played about his mouth as he thought about the risk he would take and the possible rewards. Of all the things the Black Mask had stolen, nothing would ever be as sweet as one kiss.

Seven

Rose paused on the threshold as she entered her aunt's bright and cheerful morning room. Amidst the daffodil-yellow walls and delicately spindled furniture covered with straw-colored satin, her admirers did indeed look overwhelming, as though she'd wandered into a convention of giants. She took a deep breath and smiled a welcome. There were only four of them, after all.

Colonel Wapton, rising to his feet with alacrity, only just managed to save a Sevres vase from toppling over. Mr. March looked like an overlarge puppy in a small kennel, hoping to be taken for a walk. Mr. Allen, newly elected member of Parliament, was a very earnest young man with large hands and feet. As he'd been elected on a agricultural ticket, he seemed to think it would be a betrayal of his principles to have new clothes tailored. Therefore his hands looked even larger because his sleeves were slightly too short.

Young Lord Duchan was extremely well turned out. Regrettably, the extremes of fashion did not flatter his square torso and heavy thighs. His shirt points reached to his ears, and his mouth was half muffled by a snow-white cravat.

Rose liked them all very much. She encouraged Mr. Allen to overcome his shyness and discuss his principles. She enjoyed hearing the latest news of young Lord Duchan's abundant brothers and sisters. Mr. March liked best to sit and gaze at her in awestruck admiration, which was always pleasing. And Colonel Wapton could make her laugh, causing the other three to look daggers. She liked them all and couldn't imagine being married to any of them. So far, she'd managed by exercising a great deal of tact to keep them from proposing.

"I'm sorry I couldn't be here yesterday when you called," Rose said, to a chorus of deprecation. She waved them all to their seats and held court on the sofa. Though she laughed and chatted in what she fancied was her usual style, she'd arranged herself so she could keep an eye on the gilt clock ticking merrily on the mantel. She'd instructed her aunt's cook to send up the tea tray fifteen minutes early. They'd drink one cup and be on their way in a little less than half an hour. Rose wanted the room to be clear by eleven. If Sir Niles should deign to drop in, she wanted no distractions.

Aunt Paige had promised to come down to help, but she was distracted, busy attiring herself against the arrival of her own admirer, General O'Banyon. So far, she'd rejected two gowns and was nearly in tears over the choice. Rose, too, had known unusual indecision over the choice of her clothes this morning. She didn't dare speculate on what that meant.

Finally, at ten minutes to eleven, the large men exited in a straggling line. Colonel Wapton and Lord Duchan tried to outlast each other, but when Rose stood up and thanked them for entertaining her, they had no choice but to leave in tandem.

Rose heaved a sigh of thankfulness as the door closed. Going to the mantel, she rang for the maid to take out the tray. "Please bring a fresh pot in fifteen minutes, but only two cups."

Looking up into the mirror hanging at an angle on the chimney breast, Rose wondered if the blue foulard had been the right choice. It had looked all right upstairs, but against all this yellow, didn't it look a little insipid? Well, it was past praying for. If he came at all, it would be soon. She didn't want to keep Sir Niles waiting. She wanted him in the best possible and most malleable mood.

The knock at the front door seemed to reverberate in her heart. Trying to achieve an easy pose, Rose leaned an elbow on the mantel, crossed to sit on the sofa, retired to an armchair with an improving book on her knee, all in the time it took Sir Niles to enter, doff his hat, and be escorted to the door.

The butler bowed him in and himself away. Niles saw Rose, sitting bolt upright on the edge of an armchair, her color high and her eyes round with expectation. She had apparently been reading.

"I trust I don't disturb you."

"On the contrary. I'm so happy you could come." She rose and came to meet him halfway, her hand prettily extended.

Another knock at the front door made him drop her hand a little more quickly than Niles had wanted to. He actually hadn't wanted to let go at all.

Rose gave a little laugh. "You'll be flattered to know you are more punctual than the military, Sir Niles."

"One of your admirers, Miss Spenser?"

"No. My aunt's, if you please."

With a graceful gesture, she invited him to sit on the sofa. She joined him there. He breathed in her scent of carnations and wondered at her restraint in not using rose water. Any other girl with her name, he felt, would have been unable to resist.

He wondered why he'd come after all but vowing to send regrets. Riding with Buzzy, he'd told himself he could see Rose that evening and discuss whatever it was amidst a crowd of people. Surely that was more sensible than seeing her alone. During his bath, he'd mentally sketched the note he'd send her with his regrets. At breakfast, he'd called for pen and paper, only to tear up the thing between tying his cravat and putting on his waistcoat. Then, though he'd told Baxter he was going to his club, he found himself at her door. It was like being under a spell which sapped one of all self-control.

"Sir Niles," she began breathlessly. Then the door opened and she smiled apologetically. "Tea?"

Her little fuss with the tea table, with cups and sugar, and urging him to try one of the cook's special cakes, gave him the chance to study her more closely. A little blush came and went on her cheeks as she noticed his glance. "It's always too warm in this room on a sunny day. I think it must be the color of the paint. Shall I open a window?"

"Pray don't trouble. Unless you wish me to open it for you?"

She shook her head, a lock of silky dark hair falling from her upswept arrangement. It looked as if it would curl around his hand like a friendly kitten. Niles willed himself not to reach out. He liked her in blue, with the matching ribbon threaded through her hair.

"More tea? A little more sugar?"

If she had brought him here so boldly in order to continue their flirtation, why was she treating him like a crotchety Dutch uncle? Next she'd be fetching a pil-

low for his aching back or a footstool for his gouty*
foot.

"Miss Spenser, in your note you mentioned some
serious matter you wished to discuss. May I know
what it is?"

"I hope you don't think me too forward, Sir Niles,
asking to see you alone this way. I thought for a long
time before taking this step, considering your past
reputation and my future."

"Yes, I wondered if you had considered that. I
thought about it too, but the tone of your note to me
seemed to compel my compliance."

She smiled directly into his eyes, and Niles caught
his breath. Then a tiny frown of puzzlement nestled
between her charmingly arched brows. "Why is your
reputation so bad?" she asked unexpectedly. "You
don't seem to me so much worse than other men. I
have been about this world a little now, and I am
aware that many men foster irregular relationships."

Could she read the shock in his eyes? Niles hoped
not, yet Rose faltered a little and then hurried on. "I
mean . . . one can hardly fail to be aware of such
things. The royal dukes certainly take no pains to conceal their liaisons or their baseborn children. There
are many such. There are even those who flaunt their
. . . their mistresses on their arm in public. I don't
see why you should be singled out as a particularly
wicked man. On the contrary, you seem . . ." She
closed her lips tightly.

"Comparatively inoffensive," Niles finished for her.

She nodded, a twinkle appearing in the depths of
her eyes.

"I do try to live it down," he said wistfully. "But the
ton has a long memory for folly. When I first came to
London a dozen years ago—has it been as long as

that? Let me see. I'm thirty now, almost thirty-one. Yes, quite a dozen years. How old I suddenly feel."

"No one would assume you were as old as that," Rose said.

"Thank you. At any rate, when I first came to London, I fell into some devilish scrapes—I beg your pardon."

"Don't. You should hear how Rupert speaks when he forgets I'm a girl."

"That confirms a great deal I have suspected about your brother. How could anyone forget you are a girl?" Niles read her rejection of the light compliment in the way she shrank back almost imperceptibly.

He sipped his tea to give her time to recover her poise. "I was telling you of my early indiscretions. I don't know that they were so much worse than the average young hothead finds in town. Perhaps, if anything, London is a touch milder now. The great hells have closed or been converted to gentleman's clubs. The great houses . . ."

He suddenly found it necessary to clear his throat. If it was impossible to forget that Rose was a girl, it was yet so easy to talk to her that he was tempted into saying too much. She didn't need to hear of the great whorehouses that had flourished in his youth.

"The great houses? Do you mean Carlton House?"

"Yes," Niles said, grasping at this way out of his difficulty. "Prinny's first great monstrosity. I think it could stand as the symbol of license that flourished then."

"The Pavilion at Brighton is not so very staid."

"But it's all show. Carlton House was more genuine, less of a hothouse bloom. He never should have torn it down."

"You enjoyed your first Season in town?"

"We did, ma'am. I had a cousin, you see. Almost a brother. Certainly the best boon companion anyone could ask for, with one slight exception. He had a genius for getting into scrapes and for pulling me in after him. I would start out trying to save him from his folly and wind up, more often than not, with the blame—the fame and the infamy as well."

Rose laughed. "Poor Sir Niles. Who is this engaging fellow?"

"His name was Christian. Whether that name was given to him in pious hope or as a joke of the devil remains a question in the family to this day."

"*Was* Christian? You mean he is . . ."

"We both went into the army when the Peace of Amiens fell to bits. I came out a man devoted to peace and the leisure arts. Christian perished."

Rose turned her face away. "My condolences, Sir Niles."

He slid his hand over hers. "You would have liked him. All the ladies liked him."

For a moment, she let her hand stay motionless beneath his. "Was there no special girl in his life?"

"No one for either of us. But I often thought the right girl could have gentled him. Made him less wild, less desperate. You see, he had no money at all, and it troubled him. He saw worse men rise to the top of their profession just because they had fortunes and he had none. He wouldn't take help from anyone."

And so he was tempted, and so he fell, but Niles didn't want Rose to know that. Let her think of Christian as Niles remembered him. Mad, heedless, full of fun, and a respecter of no person.

Niles took his hand away, but the pressure-memory of his touch stayed with Rose. He had spoken with such tenderness and understanding of his friend.

Surely he'd react the same way when she spoke about Rupert.

"Anyway," he said, "that is half the story of my evil reputation."

"Only half?" she asked, blinking hard, hoping he didn't notice the tears in her eyes.

"Only half. When I returned to London as an officer, well, I had little reason to practice restraint."

"Because you were afraid of being killed?"

"No. We never gave it a thought. But we were heroes, and everybody treated us well. Ladies were mad for scarlet coats, and whether we were barracked in town or the country, lasses came for miles to flirt and to dance. I remember a family of five sisters— well, the older two were interested in some wealthy neighbors, but the three youngest were the most arrant flirts in the county. Any officer was fair game."

"And you didn't flee in horror?" she said in mock surprise.

"Not at that time. There were, however, other girls who took things more seriously than I anticipated. Though no fathers came after me with shotguns, it was a near run thing a few times."

"You don't learn quickly, I take it."

"Not at that time, no. If the campaign in the south hadn't needed more officers, I should probably be married with a healthy family by now."

"Do you regret you are not?"

"At this moment, I can only be grateful."

Rose stiffened. "Please don't feel you must support your reputation with me, Sir Niles. I don't care for flirtation."

He bowed his head. "Forgive me. After so much time, it's become a reflex. Like standing up when a lady enters the room."

"That surely is to show respect. Flirting with me does not."

"I am chastened, Miss Spenser."

"You are forgiven, Sir Niles."

His smile held such understanding, such warmth of humor, that Rose truly, truly felt she could talk to him about her consuming anxiety over Rupert. He, too, had known someone who seemed to take unholy delight in worrying relations. Not that Rupert was ever terribly wicked. But he did not worry noticeably, which left her to do it for him.

She took a sip of her tea to moisten her mouth. It was not hot enough. "I shall ring for some more tea," she said. "Then I shall only take up a very few more minutes of your time."

"My time is . . ." he started to say when the morning room door opened.

Hurst, Lady Marlton's butler, entered, despite Rose's disapproving glance. "I beg your pardon, Miss Spenser. I hesitate to disturb you."

"It's quite all right," Rose said, because she couldn't very well remind Hurst she'd asked not to be disturbed, not in front of Sir Niles.

"Colonel Wapton has called again."

"Again?"

"He believes he has left an item behind." Hurst let his gaze roam over the room. "I don't espy it. The gentleman himself asks permission to search."

"Certainly," Rose said as graciously as she knew how, though she feared a tiny sigh of annoyance escaped her lips. She cast an apologetic glance at Sir Niles and saw his pose had stiffened. The contrast with the easy posture he'd had before was so great she almost thought someone had sneaked in and replaced him with a statue of himself. Only his eyes were alive, and they were frowning.

The colonel came in, talking quickly. "Please forgive this intrusion, Miss Spenser."

"Pray don't mention it," Rose said, for what else could she say? With luck, this interruption would be brief so she could return to that state of comfortable agreement she'd established with Sir Niles. "What is it you have forgotten?"

A tinge of color crept into the colonel's already bright cheeks. "My . . . my sword, ma'am. I can't think how I walked halfway to Bond Street without noticing it wasn't at my side. Ah!" Half the bulky colonel disappeared as he went down on one knee behind the sofa. Sir Niles twisted in his seat, groping for his quizzing glass in the pocket of his pale waistcoat.

Colonel Wapton rose, brandishing his enscabbarded sword. Sir Niles recoiled, saving his shoulder by inches.

"However did you come to lose it?" Rose asked after a sigh of relief.

"I removed it from the hanger when I sat down. I suppose I must have kicked it under the sofa when I stood up."

"How energetic," Sir Niles murmured.

Colonel Wapton's heavy brows closed across his forehead. "I regret I haven't the pleasure of this gentleman's name."

"Oh, I do beg your pardon. Sir Niles Alardyce, may I present Colonel Colin Wapton of the 13th Dragoons."

Without standing, Niles extended two fingers in a limp handshake. "How d'you do?"

"An honor," the colonel said curtly, a slight sneer distorting his regular features. Obviously dismissing Sir Niles as a negligible character, he turned to Rose.

"Will you save me a gavotte at Mrs. Ffolliot-Ransome's rout this evening?"

"I shall be glad to, Colonel. The first one?"

"Excellent. When will we have the pleasure of seeing you waltz, Miss Spenser?"

"Not for some time, I'm afraid."

"But you attend Almack's? I'm sure I saw you there."

"Yes, I've been permitted to step over the portal."

"Then there's no reason why you shouldn't waltz. Save me a waltz, instead?"

"I'm afraid it's impossible," she said, shaking her head. "I haven't learned the steps as yet."

"No? Whatever is your aunt thinking of? I beg your pardon, I don't mean to criticize so good a lady, but for a young lady in her first Season not to waltz . . . well, it's absurd. You should learn at once."

Sir Niles coughed gently. "Is it the army you represent, sir, or a young ladies' academy?"

The colonel glanced at Sir Niles. "It must be every gentleman's interest to see Miss Spenser never sits out a dance."

"Energetic, indeed. Quite exhausting, in fact."

Rose hurried to speak, feeling disaster in the air. "Yes, I sometimes do enjoy sitting out a dance. It's easy for you gentlemen in your pumps, but I assure you, a lady's feet begin to ache dancing in tight satin slippers."

"One should always have a care for one's feet," Colonel Wapton said. "We learn that on our first long march. Fashionable boots and shoes are worse than useless."

Sir Niles peered down at his highly polished top boots and then glanced through his glass at the colonel's. A slight spasm of distaste wrought his features. "British citizens should be made more aware of the privations suffered by their armed forces. Demmed if I shan't write a letter to the *Times* about it."

Rose could hardly believe this cynical and sneering Sir Niles was the same man to whom she'd been so close to confiding all her hopes. What had happened to change him? Nothing but Colonel Wapton's entrance. She would have a sharp word with Hurst and remind him when she left orders not to be disturbed, she didn't wish to be disturbed. It had been a kindness on Hurst's part, since the colonel couldn't appear on parade without his sword, but all the same!

But why had Sir Niles changed? He couldn't be jealous of Colonel Wapton's morning call; she had given him no cause to believe her heart was anything but independent. Nor could it be jealousy of Colonel Wapton's uniform, since he'd served himself. And it couldn't be that there was some antipathy between the two men, for she had only just this moment introduced them.

Yet from the instant Colonel Wapton had appeared, Sir Niles had changed from a kindly and amusing friend into this combination of dandy and high-nosed aristocrat.

Rose felt as if she could cry from sheer frustration. She'd come so close to asking Sir Niles to postpone demanding money from Rupert. She should have spoken up sooner instead of dallying away her time with light conversation. What wouldn't she give to have that privacy back again? But she felt even if she were alone with Sir Niles, she'd find herself with the colder, supercilious version, and she couldn't talk openly with *him.*

Colonel Wapton, having secured his sword on his person and her promise of a dance, made noises about leaving. Rose saw him to the drawing room door. "I'm frightfully sorry to leave you with such a dreary companion," he whispered. "Shall I stay and protect you?"

"You're very kind, but no," she said brightly, avoiding the intimacy of a whisper.

"Brave girl." He gave her a casual salute, two fingers waved in the direction of his forehead.

Rose closed the door behind him. She refused to give up without at least one more attempt, though she had a cold certainty at heart that she would fail. "What a foolish man," she said, returning to the sofa, her skirts rustling. "Imagine leaving his sword."

"Is he one of your admirers?"

"Oh, I doubt he's serious. I'm just someone he calls on in the morning."

As though he found it too uncomfortable to sit any longer, Sir Niles rose and walked to the window. He held back the sheer silk undercurtain with one graceful hand. "But he calls often?"

"Fairly often. Aunt Paige calls him one of my giants. I don't know why it is, but I seem to collect the most enormous men. They take up a great deal of space and nearly all the available air."

"You don't care for very large men?"

The sunlight on his dark brown hair brought out a shimmer of red highlights. It also showed with heartbreaking clarity the thinness of the skin at his temples, a pulse beating there, and the circles under his eyes. "You don't look well," she said impulsively.

"I assure you I am entirely well."

"Perhaps you aren't sleeping enough."

"You were kind enough in your note to mention my evening activities. Is this more of the same?" His voice was harsh.

"No doubt you think me very impertinent, and perhaps I am. Yet I cannot apologize for my concern for your health."

"My health is not your concern, Miss Spenser. Despite what half the females in town seem to believe, I am not perishing for want of a woman's touch in my life. I resent such meddling deeply."

Rose told herself there was no use in growing annoyed. Yet her hopes had been high since this interview had begun and now they were dashed. She couldn't help feeling disappointed. It was that feeling alone which brought the tears into her eyes.

"I beg your indulgence, Sir Niles. My concern shall not trouble you again." She stood up. "My goodness," she said with patent falseness, "is that the time? Well, I have enjoyed our chat, sir. What a pity it cannot be extended, but I know how many calls you have on your time. Half the females in London, didn't you say?"

"Half of them minus one, Miss Spenser. I should ask you to save me a dance this evening in order to give you the pleasure of refusing. But I am not so unselfish as all that."

"I can well believe it." Instead of offering him her hand, as she would to any other departing guest, she dropped a deep and ironical curtsy as he left. His bow answered hers with studied exactness.

She went to the morning room window to look out into the street. She did not pull back the curtains, as he had done, but watched through their softening veils as Sir Niles came out. He gave a flick to the brim of his tall, sloping-sided hat, setting it to a perfect angle over his eye, and held his stick under his arm at precisely the most insouciant angle. His whole bearing breathed relief. No doubt it was a relief to escape from her. No doubt the attitude of a kind friend was a difficult one to support for any length of time, so unnatural a posture. She could only wonder why he'd troubled.

"Pardon me, Miss Spenser. Lady Marlton requests you come upstairs," the butler said from behind her.

"Thank you, Hurst. I'll go up at once."

"I hope you weren't too put out by my letting the colonel come in, miss."

"No, it all turned out for the best. Don't be troubled, Hurst."

"Thank you, miss. May I take the tray away?"

"Yes, by all means." Idly, feeling rather numb, Rose watched him sweep up the crumbs, smooth out the cushion, remove all traces of Sir Niles's visit. If only it were as easy to remove the questions from her mind. Would she ever understand men?

Eight

When Rose entered Paige's bedchamber, she found her aunt sitting on the floor before the long pier glass. The mirror was tilted forward to show her aunt's face in the bottom quarter. Aunt Paige looked like an elfin child peering over the edge of a rill. There was something hesitant about her expression, as though she didn't know whether to trust what she saw.

"Aunt Paige, are you all right?" Rose said, hurrying to her side. She sank down on her knees, not knowing if her aunt had fallen or fainted.

"Oh, I don't know. I feel all topsy-turvy."

"Let me help you to your bed. Shall I ring for your maid?"

"No, no, I'm . . ." She chuckled a little and then heaved such a heavy sigh Rose thought it would never end. "I'm in love again. Isn't it dreadful?"

Rose sat back on her heels in surprise. "In love? Dreadful?"

"Oh, yes. Perfectly horrid, in fact. You've no idea what a mess it makes of things. What a mess it makes of me." She put out a trembling hand to touch the reflection of her face. "Look at her. What is left to her? Bloom gone, sweetness gone, a few miserable remains of a once considerable charm, but nothing like it was.

I could wind a man around my little finger when I was a girl. They all came flocking, you know. Half a dozen men wanted to marry me, but I had to have Richard Lethbridge."

"I don't remember him." He was only a name, a scrap of gossip overheard before someone noticed the child.

"No, he died some years before you were born. Oh, I was mad for him, absolutely out of my mind. Would you like to see his portrait?"

Rose wanted anything that would get her aunt off the floor. She looked so odd huddled there, like a savage who didn't know there was such a thing as a chair in the world. "By all means. He must have been very handsome."

"Oh, I wouldn't say so. Fascinating, though. The miniature is in the little drawer under my dressing table mirror."

"I don't like to pry. Why don't you find it?"

"It's folly to keep secrets from relations; they find them out anyway. Go on." Aunt Paige fell again to studying her face, though with no sign of greater pleasure. As though sounding for depth, she tapped along the ridge of her cheekbone, pulling back the slightly fallen skin at the edge of her eye.

Rose turned the pink tasseled key in the shining brass lock. The little drawer popped open as if spring-loaded. It was filled by several pieces of paper and two small portrait heads on ivory.

"Which one?"

"The older one."

Rose looked at the men's faces. One was graced with gray hair and the other was as fair and young as Apollo. Carrying them gingerly, she brought them to her aunt.

"There he is," Paige said, tears in her eyes. "Not handsome, no. But so kind. He married me out of kindness, though I vowed I would make him love me one day. I think he did come to it, before the end."

"Mother said once you had been devoted to your husband, but I never knew which . . ." There was no diplomatic end to that sentence.

"Oh, yes, I was devoted to Richard. He must have been all but forty when we were married. I hounded him into it; yes, I did," Paige said in response to Rose's instinctive denial.

"Everywhere he went, there I was, making sheep's eyes at him like the lovesick schoolgirl I was." Paige looked in the mirror and wore the expression of a mooncalf, eyes round, mouth hanging open, hands quivering as if with greed.

"He didn't have to marry you."

"I made myself and him so conspicuous that he was compelled to do something. And he could never bring himself to hurt such a foolish child, so he proposed. How delighted I was. How certain I could never deserve such a paragon! I started out under a crushing load of obligation and gratitude. It's a wonder we were ever happy."

"No man would marry for such a reason as that," Rose said, scoffing.

"Why not? It's more or less why I married Japhet. Once you start tripping over a man every time you turn around, you might as well marry him. Besides which, he had a title without any funds to support it and I had inherited Richard's fortune. We were destined for each other."

"I remember Uncle Japhet. He seemed very pleasant."

"Oh, he was. Always smiling, always cheerful. One

could never indulge in a fit of the sulks with him around or even a gentle melancholy. He couldn't bear to see unhappy faces, not even a maid with the toothache. I sometimes wish we could have had children together; I'm sure they would have been delightfully happy babies."

She turned again to the mirror and heaved another endless sigh. "I'm too old now, and he's bound to want children."

"Are you talking about . . . about the general?"

"Yes. Augustus O'Banyon." She rolled his name on her tongue like a candied violet from the top of a particularly delectable pastry. "He'll probably want to live in Ireland once he retires from the service. Well, it's a pretty country. They say Dublin is quite civilized now."

"But you only met him last night," Rose pointed out.

"I know. But he swears he took one look at me and knew I was his. I'd laugh at that if it weren't for feeling precisely the same way. Whatever shall I do?"

Rose had never heard of anything so romantic or more ridiculous. Surely middle-aged people like her aunt and the general should have more control over their feelings, rather than letting themselves be ridden by them like a pair of star-crossed children. She neither believed nor disbelieved in love at first sight, for surely no one had ever seen it except in plays. Perhaps it happened once in a great while, otherwise how could playwrights imagine it and audiences accept it? All the same, it sounded uncomfortable at best.

"It's like Romeo and Juliet," she said, tactfully choosing a romantic precedent.

"Oh, I do hope not. I should hate to take poison."

"No, she stabbed herself after Romeo drank the poison."

"I believe you're right. Well, that's love for you."

Now was patently not the time to trouble her aunt with her or Rupert's problems. She would have to think of some other way to nullify those pledges. Perhaps if she wrote to their father herself, pleading Rupert's cause once more, he would relent and permit Rupert to enter the army.

Though it would not end Rupert's obligation to pay Sir Niles, it would serve to keep Rupert from falling more deeply into debt. His pay would not be great, but it would be something more than he had at present.

"Is Rupert dining at home tonight?" Aunt Paige asked.

"I haven't any idea. Perhaps he said something to Hurst."

"It's only that the general has asked me to accompany him to dinner at the Great Pulteney Hotel. I don't think he'd mind if you joined us."

"No, thank you. Two's company; three's none."

"But if Rupert isn't home, how shocking that you should eat alone."

"I shall dine in state, Aunt. Besides, someone must eat here, or your cook will give notice."

Rose went on thinking about Rupert while Aunt Paige chattered away, mingling gossip with paeans of praise for her new friend. Rose needed only to nod and hum an encouraging sound from time to time.

If only there were some way to delay the necessary payment until Rupert could manage to assuage his debts. If only someone could take Rupert's vowels and hide them until he could pay. He could still acknowledge the obligation while being uncertain of the exact amount. Surely no honor code would be more than lightly bent by such methods. The intent to pay would still be there; only the time of payment would be in doubt.

Might as well wish for the sea and all its treasures. She didn't even know where Sir Niles kept his important papers. Whatever notion had crept into her thoughts about searching his house during an evening's party had to be, however reluctantly, set aside. Only a professional thief would even begin to know where the most common hiding places were. She could only think of under the bed, and Sir Niles had already said he had every intention of moving his jewels to some other location.

"I received the most diverting invitation," Aunt Paige said suddenly. "I think Augustus will escort us if I ask him."

"Go where, Aunt?"

"Catherine Yarborough's masquerade. Vulgar idea, but rather daring, too. Wednesday next, which is lucky. It will take us several days to create costumes and have them ready."

"What will you choose?" Rose felt a stir of excitement. Had she already grown so jaded with the pleasures of London that it took something like a masquerade to rouse her enthusiasm? She hoped not. She had so much still to enjoy, so many daydreams to yet fulfill.

Aunt Paige turned to the dressing table mirror and turned her head appraisingly from side to side. She seemed to be trying to see her profile in full. "Augustus suggests Antony and Cleopatra, but I think we should choose a subject that is a little more staid. I'm not a Bird of Paradise, after all."

"What about me?" Rose said, bending her knees to bring herself within the mirror's frame. She squinted a little, trying to picture herself in some other guise.

"With your dark hair and fair skin, I could see you as a Spanish Infanta or Catherine of Braganza. I have a string of pearls we could weave into your hair. It would be vastly pretty." Aunt Paige went to her jewel box and opened the lid. "That jogs my memory. Augustus says I should put my most valuable jewels in the bank for safekeeping at least until this Black Mask maniac is captured."

"Maniac?" Aunt Paige had always shown a certain ironic fascination with the burglar's exploits. This was a change of front. Rose wondered if it were the general's influence.

"Haven't you heard? He's struck again."

"No! Who?"

"Some sort of City fellow. Apparently he'd amassed a stunning collection of famous jewelry. Very influential families, they say. Must have sold off their treasures secretly and had them replaced with copies."

"And the Black Mask stole them?"

Aunt Paige pursed her lips and shook her head, apparently at the fetter-like bracelet she held in her hand. "Ghastly. How did women ever wear these things a hundred years ago? I should have the stones reset. They're quite pretty opals, though I'm not fond of opaque stones." She turned her head and smiled at Rose. "I'm sorry, my love. No, they say the Black Mask didn't get away with anything this time, not so much as a penny piece."

"A pity to take such risks for nothing."

Paige shrugged slightly. "I'd follow Augustus's advice were I not perfectly sure the Black Mask has his sights on grander treasures than I possess. Though both my husbands were ever generous, I don't have the sort of incredible jewels a true collector or a true thief would find interesting."

"I wonder how he knows which people do have such things?" Rose wondered.

"Come and sit down here, Rose. Let's try these pearls."

Still abstracted, Rose easily sat still while her aunt, and soon her aunt's maid, tried first one arrangement and then another of her hair. Finally, Aunt Paige stood back. "Definitely a Spanish princess."

Rose glanced up. They'd performed a wonderful transformation, parting her hair in the center and pulling each side up under a sheer white veil, a drape of milky pearls contrasting with Rose's dusky waves and falling in a swoop across her forehead. "I don't look like myself."

"That is the idea behind a masquerade, Rose. To be someone else for an evening. That's why they so often turn into bacchanals. People forget who they are. Clergyman become rakes, rakes become devils, chaste girls become . . . well, I think we can trust dear Catherine to keep her party from going even an inch over the line. She's rather a stickler for the proprieties."

"That's just as well," Rose said. She put down the hand mirror with which she'd been admiring the back of her head. "But I don't think I'll be a Spanish princess."

"No?" Aunt Paige said, exchanging a disappointed glance with her maid.

"No. Though the style you've given my hair is wonderful and will do for my other idea."

"Which is?"

"I shall attend as the Malikzadi, complete with ruby."

* * *

In the five days that passed, Rose saw very little of
Sir Niles. Once again, she had come to catching only
glimpses of him at parties. At a huge picnic, she saw
him playing croquet with a crowd of flower-like young
ladies, apparently receiving instruction. He sent her a
wry salute with a mallet.

On another occasion, he'd asked her to dance
rather late in the evening. She'd felt strangely tri-
umphant when she'd showed him that the small ivory
plaque of her dance card was entirely covered with
the names of more punctual and thus more fortunate
men. Her triumph fell rather flat, however, when he
seemed not to mind a particle.

Twice she sat near to him during refreshments, not
that he noticed. Both times, he had been talking to—
or, rather, listening to—a vivacious young blonde with
fascinating green eyes. Between the blonde's never-
slowing tongue and the proximity of three out of four
of Rose's largest admirers, she did not exchange a single word with Sir Niles. She vowed, however, to wish
him happy the next time they met. Rumor had it the
blonde would be Sir Niles's fate.

Yet by the time Wednesday came, she'd passed on
to a new flirt and was heard to say Sir Niles's reputation was fully deserved. Rose hoped he was ashamed
of himself, but doubted anything could pierce the
armor of his self-esteem. She hardly imagined a disappointed woman's influence could serve where the
whispers of the most important people in England
had failed.

In her desire to avoid Sir Niles, which seemed only
to lead to her seeing him everywhere, Rose almost
failed to notice that one of her admirers had unaccountably taken himself off. Despite his previous
interest in her, Colonel Wapton had ceased to call.

She wondered if Sir Niles's rudeness to him had tainted her with unpleasant associations. But she soon discovered the colonel had all but ceased going anywhere.

The one subject on everyone's tongue was, simply, the Black Mask. With Beringer revealed as a loathsome blackmailer preying like a giant leech on society, the debate over the Black Mask's morals and intentions grew ever more intense. Had he intended the revelations he'd created, or were they accidents, mere by-products of burglary?

"I have no doubt about it," the general declared at his first dinner *en famille* when Rupert introduced the subject of the day shortly after the servants had carried in all the plates and wines for the dessert course.

Waving the jewel-like fruit tart he'd selected, the general made his point. "A man could uncover such deviltry a single time purely by accident, but to do so twice is beyond the bounds of coincidence. He must have chosen those two men precisely because he knew their secrets."

"How could he?" asked Aunt Paige.

"He's probably a confederate in their doings. A burglar would prove to be very useful in scouting the territory for a blackmailer in advance of operations. Incriminating documents, compromising billets-doux, secret sins hidden away. I wouldn't be a bit surprised to find out this slaver fellow wasn't to be one of Beringer's victims and the Black Mask was supposed to collect the proof. A mistake on his part, I fancy, led to the exposure of this fat pigeon instead of leaving him ripe for the plucking."

"Oh, no, Sir Augustus," Aunt Paige protested. "I'm sure the Black Mask intended all along to uncover these evil deeds. Why, now that those two unpleasant men have been shown for what they are, if I were a criminal I wouldn't sleep at night for fear the Black Mask meant to expose me next."

"And what crimes do you have on your conscience, eh?" the general asked, leering genially across the table, his masculine appeal not a whit lessened by the smear of whipped cream on his upper lip.

Rose met Rupert's eye and stifled a giggle behind her napkin. The general conducted his lovemaking in the most straightforward way. It should be shocking, but Rose could not choose but be diverted at his antics and pleased for Aunt Paige. She, dear thing, went about in a haze of happiness, hardly aware of her surroundings, especially when the general was near. Her lovely soft eyes misty with romantic daydreams, all but forgetting her duty to her niece and nephew, Paige looked a dozen years younger than the forty she admitted to.

Rupert shook his head, but winked at Rose before continuing. "I think the Black Mask has more than a little larceny in his soul, but does that necessarily mean he can't do a bit of good in the world as well? Men like Beringer and Curtman are blots on England's ledger. Blackmail's bad as clubbing a fox, and as for slavery . . . well, I was glad to hear Curtman fled the country. Beringer won't be so lucky—or so they say."

"He'll flee the country, right enough," said the general with satisfaction. "And at government expense. He'll be transported sure as a gun. No one's going to listen to his excuses with the duchess weeping in the witness box."

"Hasn't he threatened to tell all he knows? One would think he had a thousand secrets from all those poor people he was threatening. I know I'd do anything to prevent my indiscretions from being known.

I can't imagine how the duchess can bring herself to talk about it, and in court, too."

"That's the worst thing he could do, dear Lady Marlton," Sir Augustus said shrewdly. "He would lose whatever sympathy he had with the court. I've presided at enough courts-martial to know you're halfway home if you win the sympathy of the court."

"I shouldn't imagine the judge will show him very much sympathy. I wouldn't," Paige said, cutting up an apple with bloodthirsty emphasis.

"Every little bit helps, m'dear. It's a capital charge. Only the mercy of the judge can save him from Tyburn Tree."

Rose was struck by a sudden shiver that forced her to put down her glass lest she spill the dessert wine across the shining expanse of mahogany dining table. "If they catch the Black Mask," she asked, "won't they hang him as well? He has stolen considerably more than many of those poor unfortunates who go to execution."

"Aye, he has," the general said, not unduly concerned. He spun the epergne before him slowly, searching perhaps for another fruit tart or simply mesmerized by the brilliant flicker of the candles in the gleaming silver. "But no doubt the court, should he ever face one, would consider leniency based on the good he's done, whether inadvertently or purposefully. All the same, I don't approve of a man taking the law into his own hands. We wouldn't tolerate it in the army."

"I, for one," said Rupert excitedly, "doubt they'll ever catch him. He's shown himself too clever for those clodhoppers at Bow Street. My friends feel the same way, those who've given it any thought at all. The Black Mask brings a little excitement to living in town."

"Thank you very much," Aunt Paige said. She could not maintain her austere expression for longer than it took Rupert to begin a stumbling apology. "Don't be so silly. I know exactly what you mean. Talking about the Black Mask is much more interesting than the usual chatter about who is dancing, marrying, or on the outs with whom."

Rose nodded. She could live happily for the rest of her life never hearing another word about Sir Niles and his latest conquest.

"Why, even fashion has started taking an interest in him," Aunt Paige continued. "I was at my milliners when, lo and behold, she brings out a chip hat with a black veil and calls it 'a la Masque Noir.' It's apparently the last word in style." Seeing a lack of belief on the men's faces, she applied to Rose for confirmation.

"Yes, indeed. And when we went on to buy some lace, it too was of 'the Black Mask style.' I haven't the least notion why. It was pink thread lace."

The two men began to laugh. Rose and Paige looked at each other. Men laughed at the strangest things. "Come along, my love," Aunt Paige said, dabbling her fingers in the lemon-scented water before her and wiping them on her napkin. "Let us leave Sir Augustus and Rupert to their port. I want to talk to you about your costume. It's nearly finished. I think it will cause quite a stir."

In the doorway, she paused to glance at Sir Augustus in what Rose, exiting behind her, could only think of as an intriguing fashion. Paige held herself with her body half turned toward the general, her eyelashes modestly lowered. Then she raised them slowly, turning the full force of her lustrous eyes on him.

"Don't linger too long," she said, a little more breathily than usual.

The general, still on his feet from the ladies' rising from the table, pulled his heels together smartly, bowing from the waist, his hand at the salute. "At your command, my lady."

Once in the drawing room, Rose looked with concern at her aunt. "Are you feeling well? Your voice has become quite hoarse. I noticed the candles were smoking rather a lot."

"I'm perfectly well," Aunt Paige said, smiling in that way that made Rose feel like a perfect child, and passed on to the absorbing subject of their costumes for the upcoming masquerade.

After retiring for the night, Rose posed in front of the mirror, pretending she had stopped in a doorway mimicking the pose and action of her aunt. Lips straight or only faintly smiling, head held slightly to the side, lashes slowly down, then slowly up. What was there in all that to make a man snap to attention? Perhaps it was just the way Aunt Paige did it; that and the way General Sir Augustus O'Banyon felt about Aunt Paige.

Nevertheless, Rose practiced once more, imagining she stood before a man who was falling inexorably in love with her. What emotion would transfigure a cynical expression then? Would Sir Niles drop the quizzing glass he'd raised to inspect her coldly? How had Sir Niles crept into her scenario?

Rose said her prayers with extra attention. Sir Niles had no place in those.

In the morning, Aunt Paige came into Rose's room while she was still in bed. "You don't want me this morning, do you, darling?"

"No, Aunt. Where are you going? You look very fine."

Paige ran her gloved hand over the stuff of her long

pelisse, cut into points at the hem and trimmed with green velvet braid. "I'm calling upon the duchess."

"Which duchess? Oh . . . that duchess," Rose said, enlightened.

"These calls for her husband to resign his post! Absurd. I could hardly believe what I read in the news this morning. I've been remiss in not calling up on her sooner. If I can, I shall prevail upon her to go driving with me. We shall cut down Bond Street and I shall order the top put down so everyone can see us."

"Can you wait while I dress?" Rose asked, throwing aside the coverlet. "I shan't be but a moment."

"You are very sweet. I know she would adore meeting you. She always has young people visiting her. But until I know which way the *ton* is going to swing, I think it wisest for you to wait. I will convey your regrets with some story of a slight indisposition. She'll understand. She's been a part of London society for years and years and knows all about the value of a sudden stomach grippe."

"But I don't mind what they think of me any more than you care."

"Oh, I care very much," Paige said. "Not what they say about me. I don't care about *that*." She snapped her fingers, the sound muffled by the green suede glove. "But I care what they say about you. An old widow may visit whom she pleases and no one will speak a word in censure. But a young girl on the brink of marriage must always take care. Besides, weren't you riding with Rupert this morning?"

"Yes," Rose admitted. "He's coming back at ten."

"Don't exhaust yourself. The Yarborough affair may go on until three in the morning, and it would be a shame to miss any by yawning." She patted her niece's cheek and set out.

Rose often borrowed a young mare from Benjamin Quayle, Rupert's wealthiest and wildest friend. Ever since hearing Rupert complain he hadn't been able to bring his horses down, Quayle had made him free of his stables. Any privilege of Rupert's was naturally, in his mind, extended to his well-beloved if meddling older sister. Mr. Quayle didn't seem to mind, and his grooms were grateful that the horses received extra exercise while eating their heads off in London.

Rupert had turned off the main bridle path for a moment to speak with friends. Rose continued on alone for a few hundred yards, letting the mare dawdle while she waited for Rupert to catch up.

A little farther on, a man stood on the path. Rose blinked in surprise. She hadn't noticed him earlier, so it seemed as if he'd sprung from the underbrush. No doubt some irregularity in the road had hidden him. She rode nearer, preparing to nod in acknowledgment as she passed.

Then, too quickly to be seen, he grabbed at the headstall, bringing the ambling horse to a stop. "What are you . . . Colonel Wapton?"

The tall young man looked strangely haggard as he glanced over his shoulder down the road. His eyes were sunk in his head, and black lines seemed carved beneath them. He wore several days' growth of beard, and the limp collar of his shirt under the frieze coat he wore testified to his lack of laundry.

"Are you alone?" he asked in a rapid whisper.

"No, Rupert is with me. What are you doing here? What is the meaning of this?" She wanted to ask *Why do you look like this?* but didn't dare. He looked hagridden, hunted, and dangerous.

"I had to see you."

"You could have called at any time."

"No, I couldn't." He glanced down the road again. Rose was glad to hear the echo of hoofbeats. "I have no right to ask any favors of you," Colonel Wapton said. "I had hoped . . . one day . . . but never mind that now. Can you meet me here tomorrow? The same time?"

Something in his haunted eyes made her agree. It was the same impulse that led her to give a hungry child a penny for a bun. "I don't know. Not the same time. I shall be later than this. There's a masquerade tonight."

"I'll wait." He seemed to melt into the bushes beside the bridle path as Rupert called the "view-halloo" from behind Rose.

"Whatever are you dawdling about for?" he asked. "Let's have a real run!"

"I should like it above all things," Rose said, aware Colonel Wapton must be watching her. In the instant before she clapped her heels to the mare's side to follow Rupert, already well away, she saw the colonel's desperate eyes staring at her from the depths of the bushes.

Nine

Rose faced a stranger in the mirror. Her long, gently waving hair had been parted in the center and allowed to fall unimpeded over the robe of stiffened red silk. The high collar made her neck look longer than ever, while the intricate black and gold embroidery along every edge of the costume added a sumptuous gleam to her gestures. But the scandalous touch that set Aunt Paige to laughing with delight and Rupert to scowling in brotherly disgust were the trousers.

"Oh, come, Rupert," Aunt Paige said while Rose stood by feeling like an overdressed doll. "They're hardly as wicked as you make out. Men wear far more revealing clothing every day of their lives."

"It's hardly the same thing. Inexpressibles are *de rigueur* and always will be. But those . . . those . . ." He stuttered a little and then stood upon his dignity. "As her brother, I think it's outrageous."

"Rupert, you're acting like an old maid," Rose said. "You can't even see my ankles, and girls have been wearing their skirts higher than that for the entire Season. I hardly think my underpinnings are going to cause much of an uproar." Only a very few inches of the tightly wrapped satin trousers were visible under the long robe, and they were the same soft red silk.

So, indeed, were the slippers, complete with curled toes.

"Actually," Rose said upon further consideration of her reflection, "I show much less of myself in this than I do in my usual ball dresses. At least one can't see so much of my bosom."

Rupert rubbed his temples. "I suppose it's useless for me to forbid you to leave the house."

"Don't be so Gothic," Aunt Paige said. "You sound as if you should be a grandfather, born sometime in the sixties and more censorious than a church full of Puritans. I know. Our father was just like that."

"Of course, I defer to your judgment, Aunt," Rupert said. "You are the only judge of what is suitable for Rose. But I'm dashed if I like it. My friends are going to be there tonight. What are they going to think when they see m'sister swanning about in that frightful rig-out? You don't even have a mask."

"Show him your veil, Rose."

Rose lifted a sheer length of red silk from the end of the bed and laid it over her hair. Then she swathed the extra length over her nose and pinned it at the side with a tiny golden pin headed with a small ruby.

"There," Paige said. "No one will recognize her."

Rupert appealed to his sister. "Come on, old girl. Put on a decent dress. You've bought half a dozen pretty ball dresses since we've come up to town."

"It's a masquerade," Rose reminded him. "What role would I be playing? The bumbling country cousin?"

"You can wear a loo mask and a domino and look charming. Most of the other girls will be wearing the same thing. You won't stand out a particle. Won't that be more comfortable than having everybody staring and whispering?"

She just gazed at him, the same obstinate firmness to her mouth she'd used whenever he'd cajole her in the nursery.

"I can't wear a loo mask because you borrowed mine," Rose pointed out sensibly.

Then she took a deep breath and confessed to them both, "I don't care to look like everyone else. I want to be unique, special, and fascinating. I want every man there to swarm about me like bees to a hive. I want to come home with four proposals of marriage and at least one of an indecent nature."

"Brava!" Paige said, clapping her hands. "Excellent. You'll be engaged before the evening is out!"

Rupert paled. "What would Mother say if she could hear you two now?"

"Heaven knows, Rupert. But I know we're going to be terribly late if you don't hurry into your costume."

"I can't wait to see it," Rose said gently, throwing him a crumb of comfort. She would have had to be insensible not to have heard him and his valet discussing ways and means to outfit him for tonight. The main secret was yet to be revealed, but Rose's maid had been constantly appealed to for various small things that appeared on a ladies' vanity.

Even when he finally emerged from the hands of his man, there was nothing to be seen of Rupert's costume except a dashing smile. For the rest, he was swathed, neck to ankles, in a black domino cloak.

"That's not fair," Rose said. "I can't criticize you as you did me."

"You'll just have to wait and see." He came farther into the drawing room where Rose was waiting. "Where's Aunt Paige gone?"

"Her hair needed another pin." Rose heard her aunt's step and stood up. She didn't tell Rupert she had found her trousers just as shocking as he had the first time she'd put them on. But neither did she mention she found them extremely comfortable.

Stepping into the carriage, for instance, though her long robe was very like a dress, she felt less in need of the footman's hand to balance her as she put her foot on the carriage step. Dancing would be interesting, she thought.

"I didn't compliment you enough on your costume, Aunt," Rose said as Paige slipped in beside her. "You look wonderful."

"You don't think it's too much?" she asked anxiously. "I'm not a young girl anymore."

"But you're not a dowager either."

"No, thank heaven." Aunt Paige smiled and gave a discreet tug to her neckline. "A shepherdess wouldn't have been my first choice, but when Miss Abrahms said she couldn't do Queen Elizabeth in time, I had few options. Besides, you are exotic enough for two. I shall reconcile myself to shepherding you."

Considering Aunt Paige's costume made the most of her creamy rounded breasts and trim waist, attractions this year's fashions largely ignored, Rose wondered if she wouldn't be shepherding ravening wolves away from her chaperon.

When they arrived, however, Rose realized she'd been foolish. General Sir Augustus O'Banyon was more than capable of protecting his prize. He had chosen to wear his uniform, glittering with every order he'd won in a long career, with a mask. His red hair and accent were very much in evidence.

"Here's a damnable thing," he growled. "I knew the young men of Britain weren't capable of much imagination. Who wants 'em to be? Following orders has brought us to where we are today. But one would hope they'd show a trifle of initiative."

"Why, Sir Augustus, you're in a pother," said Aunt Paige, perhaps a little put out he'd not noticed her costume. "What's amiss?"

Just then, Rupert came up, throwing back his domino.

"Good gad, it's another of 'em!"

At the top of the staircase that lead down into Mrs. Yarborough's ballroom, Rose felt as though she could make a similar exclamation.

Out of the hundred or so men present this evening, at least half of them had chosen to come as The Black Mask. The floor looked as if ink had been poured on it. Some men were in full formal attire, only with black shirts added to their black coats and breeches. Others had chosen a more adventurous, even piratical look, wide black shirtsleeves and sashes adding a Spanish note. Some wore capes, others many-caped coats like highwaymen. A few wore broad-brimmed hats, but everywhere she looked she saw black masks and Black Masks.

"Oh, dash," Rupert said from beside her. With his tall, lean physique, he could carry off his extremely debonair version of shirtsleeves and black Inexpressibles. His sash was red, which made his waist look very tapered beneath his wide shoulders.

"Never mind, dear." Rose said. "You're the best of them all."

"So I should hope." His despair that his costume had been copied on such a wide scale faded after a moment. "Oh, good gad, there's Sir Percy Gore-Harbridge. He's as fat as a flawn. Can you imagine him swooping through a lady's bedroom window? She wouldn't know if he were there to raid her jewel case or her larder."

"Will you be able to find your particular friends?" she asked, knowing once he'd done his duty dances, he'd be off with his cronies.

"Yes. We've all agreed to wear a touch of red about our persons. We knew, of course, that others would have the idea besides us, but obviously not on this absurd scale." He gestured at the crowd below. "Well, at least my sister will be unique. Come along, love. You've promised me a gavotte or something, haven't you?"

After they danced together, Aunt Paige joined Rose, looking rather flushed and very happy.

"I thought you'd be dancing with Sir Augustus," Rose said, finding a seat along the wall with the other young ladies and their chaperones. She saw the envious glances cast at her costume by the pierrettes, medieval maidens, and milkmaids. No single costume had struck the feminine imagination the way the Black Mask had obsessed the males.

"I may occasionally be remiss in my duties at a party where everyone is known to me, but not at a masquerade. The company can be so very mixed and not everyone behaves themselves. Especially once the champagne starts flowing."

"It reminds me of a child's birthday I once attended. I went as Elaine, the Lily Maid of Astolat. Everything went very well until the tea was served. Then the boys became all but uncontrollable."

Paige hushed her. "Never say this is like a child's party. Mrs. Yarborough thinks she's been so daring." She tapped Rose's knee with her fan. "Don't look now, but a Black Mask is coming over to ask you to dance."

"It's pointless to tell me not to look, Aunt. I wouldn't know which one you meant anyway."

Rose felt a little flutter of excitement in her breast as the gentleman in black approached. She willingly laid her ruby-laden hand in his after he received permission from Paige.

"A magnificent ring, ma'am," he said with a rather snuffy voice. Rose thanked him and chattered away about the ring, inflating its value in a very vulgar way, but she had a reason.

Rose's excitement died, only to be revived with the next applicant for her hand. She wanted to be certain every Black Mask she danced with noticed her ring. Though she doubted the one true Black Mask was present tonight, he obviously had methods to discover what went on in the houses and, more interestingly, the heads of the *ton*. Let even a few gossips find her ring interesting, and perhaps the Black Mask would try to steal it. If he did, she had him just where she wanted him.

Every one of the young ladies waiting for partners knew her, just as she knew them. She liked several of them and drifted into a little knot with them after a few dances. It was constantly changing members as men asked this one and that one to dance and then returned them. The girls admired her costume, fingering the silk, but wondered how she'd come to think of such a thing. That was her chance to talk naturally about her ring. They admired it, too, more for the tales she wove about it than for its beauty.

"Have you ever seen such a crush?" Ariadne Belmont asked, returning from a dance with a Mephistopheles for a change.

"Never in my life," Rose answered with a chorus of agreement from the other girls.

"When do we go to supper, do you suppose? My feet hurt in these shoes." Usually brunette, she wore a yellow wig whose braids hung to her waist and a circlet of oak leaves around her waist. Otherwise, she was attired as any young lady in her first Season at a ball, yet claimed to be a Saxon maiden. She was a very pleasant and fun-loving girl who, unfortunately, was the second of six daughters. There was literally not an extra shilling to be had at her house.

"I don't know, but it must not be far off. By the time we came up to the house, it was not much later than half past ten. I can't think how the grooms and drivers are managing tonight. So many carriages in the streets."

"Well, I'm not going in to supper with that devil," Ariadne declared. "He stepped on my feet worse than anyone yet."

"It must be Aubrey Dennison," Rose deduced. "No one dances worse than he does, and he's about that tall."

"Oh, then I'm certainly not going in with him. All he wants to talk about is Jessica Howe. They're going to be engaged as soon as she comes back from the seaside. Poor thing. When she had the green sickness, she lost all her color."

"I wish there were more color here," Rose said, looking again at all the black costumes. "At least Mephistopheles is all in red."

"And the pierrots are all in white. The harlequins are colorful, though."

Rose dropped her voice. "Here comes my brother to dance with you, Ariadne."

"Oh? Where?" She looked where Rose nodded at the tall young man with the scarlet sash around his waist. "I like your brother. He's cheerful. Tell him to ask me to supper, won't you?"

Rose waved subtly to Rupert, who hurried over after

bidding his friends farewell. "Monsieur Black Mask, may I introduce a Saxon maiden? Unfortunately, a wandering vagabond burned her cakes and she has none to eat. Can you aid her once the gong sounds?"

The tall man bowed and offered Ariadne his arm. Only after they'd gone off together did Rose realize that she'd seen a tiny scar at the edge of the man's well-formed mouth. He couldn't have been Rupert. She would have to find Ariadne later to find out whom she'd eaten with.

Alone for a moment, Rose glanced back toward the row of gilt chairs against the wall. Aunt Paige was deep in conversation with some other older women. So much for her attention to duty. Rose smiled tenderly and turned toward her other friends.

She never knew what instinct made her look off in the distance, across the quadruple line of the dancers. Perhaps she had felt his eyes upon her, their intent focus like a touch. They seemed to blaze as he realized she was gazing back.

Like so many others, he wore all black. But where their clothes were obviously new or adapted for the purpose of the evening, his looked . . . right. He wore a long vest over his black shirt, what appeared to be dyed riding officer's breeches, and tall boots with a dull gloss. That alone marked him as different from the other men, worldly creatures who would sooner wear bonnets than unpolished leather.

Rose felt no need to move as he started to circle around the dancers. He was coming to find her and he would find her, even if she ran away. The Black Mask could find anyone, it seemed, even those who only dreamed of him. She closed her eyes, feeling a trifle dizzy. Yet she knew the instant he appeared before her.

The mask seemed to be part of his face, almost able to move like his skin. "Will you dance?" he asked huskily.

"No. I want to talk to you. I want . . ." Some sense of self-preservation remained to her so she didn't speak all she thought, not here. "It's terribly hot in here."

"The terrace is that way."

"Yes, I know." She took his hand, gloved in worn leather, and it came to her even more strongly than when she'd first seen him that he was the one real and true Black Mask. She should have been very frightened. Inside, she felt a trembling, but it wasn't fear—unless it was fear for him. Imitate him they might, talk about him, make him a hero, but if anyone guessed as she had guessed, they'd hang him.

"You were mad to come here." She felt compelled to say it, though it was not what she wanted most to say.

"I had to come," he said.

"But why?"

He chuckled soundlessly. "I didn't know. Until . . ."

"Until?"

With a swift glance around, he led her out into the garden at the rear of the house.

Well-camouflaged among the general conglomeration of Black Masks, Sir Niles had watched as Rupert escorted Rose downstairs as soon as they'd arrived. He'd been waiting for her, all the while denying to himself that was what he was doing. But the happiness he felt when he'd identified her in her exotic Indian costume was a clue he couldn't ignore.

Besides, she looked adorable. He hadn't realized her hair was so long or so lush. The bright red color

of the silk flattered her far more than the more insipid colors then à la mode. The veil over her
delightful little nose lent her an air of mystery at odds
with her straightforward personality. He wondered if
her clothes affected her thinking the way his Black
Mask costume seemed to affect his. When he put on
those clothes, he wasn't staid Sir Niles Alardyce,
whose days of adventure lay behind him. No, he was
the avenging Black Mask, daring, dangerous, determined.

As the evening continued, as he watched her dancing with other men, laughing into their eyes, he
found it harder and harder to stay the civilized Sir
Niles. He wanted to take her out of the increasingly
stuffy ballroom, out into the night. He would show
her his London, the rooftops, the shadows, the hidden corners that gave access to secret worlds.

Sir Niles told himself that little Rose Spenser, shel-
tered innocent, would be appalled and frightened
should he ever reveal any part of what he had done.
She could never understand his need for justice,
stronger even than his desire for vengeance. Outside
the law, he'd collected his evidence, which had sent
two men deservedly to ruin.

Despite all his arguments that bade him be gone,
when Rose had seen him, his good intentions had
shattered. He craved being with her, talking to her,
even if only as a mysterious stranger. When she'd
readily agreed to leave in his company, again he was
torn. Did she feel this strange need, too? Or had he
misjudged her? Would she have left with any man who
asked her?

Then her concern for him struck him to the heart,
and both sides of his spirit stopped struggling against
the inevitable.

Niles kept her from stepping off the white stone terrace. She didn't try to shake off his hands on her shoulders. "Wait. Your eyes will adjust in a moment."

The garden was long and narrow, with a white chip path down the center and tall conifers in pots standing along the walls on either side. Benches were interspersed between the trees, some already occupied. A soft brushing sound filled the air as two or three couples walked slowly down the path, the women's antique gowns brushing over the gravel. Time seemed to have slowed almost to the stopping point, for this moment might have existed a hundred years ago or a thousand or for always.

Niles turned Rose toward him, feeling no resistance in her pliant body. The light from the ballroom, ablaze with candles, filtered through to show her face. "Why did you say I shouldn't have come? Who do you think I am?"

"I know who you are." Her whisper was as husky as his. It seemed to play along his nerves like brushing feathers. "You're the Black Mask. Have you come to steal?"

"Yes, that's why I came."

"Tonight? But Mrs. Yarborough is wearing her best necklace. I saw it."

"A necklace? No, not that." He lifted his hand and unfastened the tiny jeweled pin that secured her veil. The smooth silk slipped off the shining satin of her hair. She pushed her hair behind her ear, looking up at him with sweet confusion, her lips parted as though on a word she didn't speak.

"I came for this," he said, holding up the pin. "And for this."

Niles knew what he wanted was wrong, but he couldn't resist this attraction any longer. He cupped her face in his hands, searching her expression for any sign of what she wanted. Her eyes shone. She slid her hands over his, slipping them slowly up his sleeves.

Even Niles couldn't tell which of them kissed first. He only knew he had a vibrant woman in his arms who, though obviously inexperienced, possessed all the depths of passion he'd been longing for. He saw the danger and disregarded it, drugged by the power of a kiss. He wrapped his arms around her, pulling her so close, yet not as close as he wished.

After that first kiss, he drew her to the shadows at the side of the terrace. She followed him willingly, letting him put his arms around her again. Dropping her head onto his shoulder, she heaved a sigh so full of contentment that he all but proposed on the spot. But he had too much to explain first.

"Rose . . ."

"You know my name?"

"Of course."

Did he see her smile or did he feel it? "Rose, I have so much to tell you."

"I don't care what you've done."

"I had good reasons. And I'm afraid what I have still to do may hurt you. Tell me . . ."

"Nothing you could do will hurt me," Rose said, then hesitated. "Unless it's Rupert. Is it?"

"No, he has absolutely nothing to do with it."

"Good. Speaking of Rupert . . ."

A noise made Niles turn his head. Several dowagers had emerged from the ballroom. He tried to shield Rose from their far-seeing eyes. Their voices, ringing like a sergeant major's on the parade ground, destroyed the mood of the garden. Cupid fled in self-defense, defeated at close range by their lorgnettes.

"My, isn't it damp out?"

"Eh? Yes, very damp. You there. Girl. Go inside before you catch your death." One of them came right up to Niles and Rose. "Didn't you hear me, child? It's too damp to be flitting about gardens in those silly rags girls wear today. Not that the men have much more sense. Where's your coat, sir? In my day, men knew better than to show a lady their shirtsleeves. What are you made up as, anyway?"

Niles stood his ground as Rose, showing a sad tendency to giggle, hurried past him. He knew the old parrot lecturing them, had known her ever since he'd first come to town. Maud Margaret had been one of those most fond of Christian but always giving more good advice than any mortal man could take.

Now she was peering at him and calling to her two friends. "Come here, Alamira, Beattie. Look who it is."

With a premonition of disaster, Niles looked to discover whether Rose had gone out of earshot. She was just passing inside when Maud Margaret screeched, "It's that nice Alardyce boy."

Ten

Horrified and humiliated, Rose rushed down to the cloakroom. Alone in the peaceful room, warmly scented by the perfumes applied by guests, Rose stumbled to sit down on a bench near the door.

Sir Niles, she thought. *How could he?* To play so cruelly upon her dreams merely to steal a kiss passed the bounds of decency. How had he guessed she was one of the Black Mask's most fervent admirers when she hadn't even known it herself until just now?

Rose pressed her cool hands to her burning hot face. "What a hussy he must think me?" she muttered. He had every cause. She'd not uttered a word of protest when he had kissed her. Nor had she so much as hinted he should call upon her guardian, however temporary or distracted, to obtain permission for a betrothal. No, not she. She'd hung in his arms like a jade, behavior made all the worse by her belief at the time that she was closely embracing a wanted criminal.

A moan of despair escaped her lips. She should return home at once to bear the disgrace as she might. Those three old women, birds of ill portent comparable to the three witches in *Macbeth,* must surely have recognized her. The tale would be all over London by tomorrow. Her only hope was Sir Niles would do the honorable thing and pretend he had been proposing.

She had no intention of holding him to such a promise but without it, she would be lost.

Blindly she returned to Aunt Paige, holding her veil to her temple. She didn't seem to have noticed her niece's lengthy absence. Rose had to twitch at her aunt's voluminous skirt in order to capture her attention. "I've lost my pin," she said, showing her that the veil fell if she took her hand down.

"So you have." Paige took one from her bodice lace. "Are you enjoying yourself?"

"Oh, yes," Rose said, forcing lightness into her tone. "It's far and above all the parties we have been to yet."

"You looked a trifle flushed," Paige said, peering at her more closely as she pinned the silk. "Perhaps you should take a turn on the terrace at the rear of the house. It must be cooler there."

"Certainly." Rose smiled, though she had to swallow hard to do it. "Won't you come with me?"

"No, thank you. Augustus is certain to ask me. It's a bit of a scandal, but if you go alone and stay on the terrace, no harm can attach to you."

"Oh, I don't think I'll risk it. I'm truly not over-warm. This silk is wonderfully cool."

"I'm sorry you were gone," Paige said. "Sir Niles came to solicit us for supper."

"He did?" She spoke too loudly. The chaperones and wallflower girls all looked at her. She gave them a little half wave, a mere twiddle of the fingers. "What was he wearing?"

"Wearing? I don't know. The same as every other man here, I fancy. Though I must say, Sir Niles wears everything with such flair that one can forgive him for not taking a risk. He's always the epitome of what is correct."

Rose gazed off into the distance at a large basket of

spring flowers. What did she believe? Had she been in the arms of the Black Mask? Or was the blow-hot blow-cold Sir Niles once again favoring her with his attention? Trying to work it out, she lived again the wonder of her first kiss. It made her shiver with remembered delight.

"Now you are too cold?" Paige asked.

Rose hardly heard her. She supposed she should have been more missish, made some protest when he'd taken her outside, but she'd been rapt. All her romantic longings had seemed to coalesce around the dark figure leading her astray.

"Did Sir Niles say that he would return?"

"No, but he certainly gave me that impression. I believe," Paige said, lowering her voice, "I believe he is much taken with you. He paid you quite the nicest compliment."

Because she was so obviously waiting for her to ask, Rose made an inquiring noise.

"He said he could imagine no other company he'd prefer, that you were the liveliest girl in London and if he couldn't have supper with you, he'd sit alone."

"Highly flattering," Rose said, wondering how the endlessly correct and proper Sir Niles ever brought himself to woo the Incomparables he'd so often squired. Perhaps women of pleasure didn't require pretty speeches, only deep pockets.

Paige pondered something, lines between her brows. "I wonder if it's quite proper to call you lively. It sounds a bit hurly-burly to me."

"Only compared to Sir Niles himself," Rose said. The more she spoke with Paige, the more she convinced herself it could not possibly have been Sir Niles who kissed her. He'd never demean himself by kissing a girl in a garden. The imagination boggled at the image of the impeccable gentleman risking a scratch on his gleaming boots.

Remembering the scuffed condition of her bewitcher's boots, Rose found it impossible to reconcile that image with Sir Niles. The hair was similar, but the lines of the mouth were very different—or so she thought. She hadn't been studying details at the time.

Perhaps the elderly woman had been wrong when she'd called Sir Niles's name. There was an undoubted resemblance, but their little corner of the terrace had been quite dark. It couldn't have been him.

"Aunt Paige, does Sir Niles have any close relations?"

"I believe his mother is still residing in Bath. She suffers from some disease of the lung, and the waters are supposed to be of benefit to her. She is a Scotswoman, or so I have heard."

"No brothers? No twin, for example?"

"No. He has a sister, I think. Or is it two?" Paige slanted a glance at her. "Why this passion to know about Sir Niles's family? Are you considering increasing it?"

"Of course not. He interests me; he's such a strange combination of characteristics."

"He's a man, my dear. Trying to understand them is like trying to understand God. You're defeated before you start. One can only have faith that all will be made clear at some future time." She looked up and smiled brilliantly. "Here comes Augustus."

Rose was glad to see the general had brought Rupert with him. Perhaps it wasn't precisely done to go into supper with a brother but at least she knew who he was.

Aunt Paige said they should give Sir Niles a moment more to join them. Sir Augustus seemed to live on air when Aunt Paige was near but hinted that, having spent the last hour arguing tactics with another general, he could use a glass of champagne.

"Rupert," Rose said in an urgent undertone, "what is Sir Niles wearing tonight?"

"I haven't seen him since we arrived. Why?"

"I'm afraid I won't recognize him."

"Just don't embarrass me," he said, his earlier charity with her seemingly evaporated. "You do tend to be awfully rude to him, considering he's shown nothing but the greatest tolerance for us, a couple of nobodies from the country."

"We are not nobodies," Rose said. "Our father . . ."

"Is a banker, not a nobleman. It's dashed nice of people to show us any consideration."

"What are you talking about, Rupert? Who?"

"Sir Niles playing cards with me. Benjy Quayle lending me, and you, his horses. Mrs. Yarborough inviting us tonight."

"She is Aunt Paige's friend. Besides, I don't call fleecing you out of IOUs being particularly kind."

"Susan Yarborough . . ." Rupert muttered, apparently not attending.

"Who? Our hostess's name is Catherine."

Rupert blinked and returned to earth. "Yes, I believe you're right."

"Then why did you say Susan?"

"Did I? Slip of the tongue, that's all."

"Sir Niles!" Aunt Paige called, waving her fan. The ballroom had begun to empty as people went in search of refreshment. Rose had all the opportunity she could wish to watch him cross the floor.

As usual, his clothing could only be called faultless, a word not usually applied to costumes. He wore a proper coat, molded to his frame, a pair of proper black knee breeches, black stockings, and proper evening shoes with embroidered toes. Only in the wearing of a black shirt did he vary the attire of a perfect, proper gentleman. At every point, from perfection of fit to excellence of condition, he differed from the man who had kissed her on the terrace.

As he bowed over Rose's hand, she saw a sapphire pin glinting in the depths of his black cravat, the merest flicker of blue giving the stone away. It was the same dancing blue light she sometimes saw in the depths of his eyes. Had she seen that scintillation in the eyes of her unknown hero? Thinking back, she knew it had been too dark to see the color of his eyes.

"A pleasure to see you, Miss Spenser, as always," he said.

"You don't choose to wear a mask, Sir Niles."

"I have nothing to hide," he said, as if it were the merest commonplace. She couldn't be certain if he were giving her a hint or not. "Also, it is time for unmasking."

"Is it?" She glanced around. Masks were indeed being removed. She saw the tall man with the red sash, whom she'd mistaken for Rupert. Without the mask, he was just another attractive young man, though Ariadne, still at his side, looked up at him with newfound stars in her eyes.

"Permit me?" Sir Niles whisked away the pin that held her veil. Rose looked at him with startled eyes. So similar an action, yet so different a feeling.

Surely if he had been the man who'd kissed her, he'd show some sign. An extra squeeze of her hand, a certain possessiveness in his attitude, something! But so far as she could tell, and she was on the watch for the slightest deviation from normal, he treated her exactly as punctiliously as ever.

As they ate the delectable lobster patties and
creamy asparagus soup laid out for their midnight
feast, Rose watched Sir Niles carefully. Try as she
might she could never be certain whether what she'd
seen of the man who had kissed her matched Sir
Niles's mouth and chin.

Aunt Paige gave her a nudge with her elbow. "Stop
staring at Sir Niles, Rose. You'll make him self-con-
scious."

"Not him," she muttered. "He couldn't be more at
ease."

It was the not knowing that drove her quite mad.
The unknown one's voice had been low and husky,
but no different than Sir Niles's should he choose to
disguise it. Perhaps the other man had been a trifle
younger, but how to tell by moonlight? Rose began to
feel the only way to solve her conundrum would be to
kiss Sir Niles.

Looking at him, Rose couldn't imagine herself re-
sponding in such an unrestrained fashion to him. True,
sometimes she liked him very much. She'd even asked
herself what she would do if his partiality for her continued to the point of a proposal. Certainly she could
imagine less congenial people to be married to. But
then again, sometimes she could imagine no one
worse. All too often his frigid demeanor had repelled
her. She had only to think of his behavior toward poor
Colonel Wapton to remember him at his worst.

Strange how she had only to believe she could
never imagine kissing him to find herself imagining
just that. Now, as she looked at him at the precise moment he turned his face toward her, she felt a blush
start, as brilliant a red as her attire.

He smiled at her. "I begin to fear I have a smut on
my face."

"No. You are just as always. Perfect."

"You say that as though you disapprove. Should I spend less thought on my clothing?"

"You will think and do exactly as you wish without reference to me. I will save my breath to cool my porridge."

"I knew you to be an inestimable woman as soon as we met. Tell me, do you talk a great deal at the breakfast table?"

"I generally take breakfast in my room."

"With every word, you lead me to believe your husband will be the most fortunate of men. Is there a great deal of hunting in your part of the country?"

"Some, Rupert will know. I don't hunt myself."

"No, but others hunt you, I'm certain of it. As I learned the other day from your aunt, you have the political, the nobility, and the military calling upon you."

Rose sent a less than warm glance toward her aunt. "I don't take a count of those who find me pleasing, Sir Niles. Pray spare me your enumeration."

"Oh, but I must count myself among your admirers, Miss Spenser. You continue to please my sense of proportion and dignity."

"I do?" She wished she could decide whether she liked him or not. When he was kind, or teasing as now, she did like him. Something in her responded to the warmth of his smile and the laughter in his eyes. She liked his expressive eyebrows and the way he tucked the corners of his mouth back when he waited for her answers.

"You weren't very kind to one of my admirers the other day, Sir Niles. Colonel Wapton meant no harm."

The laughter faded out of his eyes. He looked past her. "Oh, look. Do you see the girl in the sky-blue dress?"

"The one with the feathers?" She was certain he'd looked away in search of something to distract her only after she'd raised the specter of the colonel, but it had been done so quickly, she couldn't be sure.

"That's Mrs. Yarborough's daughter."

"Is her name Susan?"

"Why, yes. Have you met her?"

"No. But I'd like to."

Half an hour later, when dancing resumed, Rose realized she'd been very skillfully steered away from any possible topic through which she could introduce Colonel Wapton. Could this be jealousy? She'd dismissed the notion before, but now it came back, bearing evidence. She would discuss the notion with Aunt Paige when, as was their habit, they stayed up after a party, analyzing what had happened, who wore what, and how many partners Rose and other girls had danced with.

Sir Niles was on the point of asking her to dance but Sir Augustus broke into his carefully considered and beautifully worded request. "And here I am, hoping for the favor myself. You don't mind, Alardyce? Privilege of rank and all that."

"Not at all, sir. Miss Spenser should always avail herself of the opportunity to dance with one of Wellington's officers. Dancing is an important part of tactics, for both sides." He bowed and withdrew, but only to a certain distance. Rose could see him standing in the midst of other men dressed as the Black Mask. He stood out like a black rose among ashes.

"Peculiar fellow, Alardyce," the general said. "Good officer, but with a deuced romantic streak. Undoubtedly gets it from his relations. Scots, some of them."

"I always thought the Irish were the great romantics, sir."

The general preened, tugging his collar and shooting his cuffs. "We manage, m'dear. We manage."

Now that she'd dismissed the idea of Sir Niles being the man who had kissed her, Rose knew she had another problem. On the one hand, as she believed, the man had been the one true Black Mask. In which case, she'd given the first kiss of her life to a criminal, and he hadn't even needed to steal it. She was also prey to the frightening suspicion she'd given her heart away as well.

If, however, the man on the terrace was not the real Black Mask, then she'd kissed a stranger, one who might still be in the ballroom. He'd known who she was, for he'd called her by name. He hadn't been tall enough or wide enough to be any of her giants. So who had she kissed? Was he, now that the unmasking had taken place, boasting of his achievement?

Trying to look twenty different ways at once, dazzled by the hot burning candles, she began to feel dizzy. Rose hadn't the heart to give in to the headache burning behind her eyes, not when Rupert, Aunt Paige, and the general were having such a good time.

The general, whom she was beginning to think of as Uncle Augustus, danced with her, showing an unexpected sense of grace.

"I wonder if I may ask a forward question, Miss Spenser."

"Ask away."

"Do you believe it too early to ask your aunt to be mine?"

"Why, I . . ."

"Your brother seems to think so," he added glumly, executing a turn with absentminded perfection.

"Did you ask him?"

He nodded. "He feels people of our years, with so

many responsibilities, shouldn't leap into matrimony without due consultation of all interested parties."

"Rupert said that?"

Augustus grinned. "Actually, he said, 'Dash it, haven't you enough on your plate without a wife? Don't know if m'father'd care for it, either.'"

Rose laughed. As the dance ended, she tucked her hand into the crook of his arm and strolled with him. "Do you care so much for our opinion? Rupert can barely manage his own affairs and I . . . seem to spend much of my time in a muddle."

"What's amiss, then? If an old soldier can be of any help to a young lady like yourself, you've only to ask."

Rose was tempted. He was a man of the world, after all, and could tell her so much she needed to know. But after a moment's reflection, she shook her head. "No, there's nothing."

"Nothing? Or nothing you can tell me?"

"Oh, Uncle . . . I mean, Sir Augustus . . ."

He pressed her hand. "No need to fly your colors. Your little slip is the best hope you could offer me."

"Surely Aunt Paige herself has not been remiss in her encouragement." Was that giving away too much of her aunt's confidence?

"She has doubts," he said. "She claims I am too impetuous, making her an offer after knowing each other such a little time, but I think she is afraid of being a widow again. Losing husbands twice is damned disheartening, I fancy."

"You've never married?"

"No. Never had the time and, in truth, I never saw a woman worth the time until I met Paige. Now I'm waiting for the chance to make her happy."

Ignoring the people around them, Rose went up on tiptoe to kiss the general's weatherbeaten face. "If all you want is to make her happy, I think I can promise no one in her family will place any objection in your way. I know that is all anyone wants for her."

"Thank you, m'dear. I hope and pray it'll not be long before you can call me 'Uncle' without miss-peaking yourself."

Eleven

By the time their carriage was extricated from the morass of others in front of the Yarborough home, three o'clock had long since struck. Despite the lateness of the hour, Rose couldn't bring herself to go to bed. An hour after coming home, she still sat up in her room, a book open, unread, on her lap.

Even though everyone should have been asleep, Rose didn't feel too surprised when someone tapped lightly at her door.

"I saw the light," Paige said, similarly attired in a wrapper. "Is anything troubling you?"

"Not at all," Rose said, dissembling. How could she admit that sleep stayed far from her because she didn't know if she was in love with a thief? "I have to be up early to go riding, so there's no point in going to sleep, is there?"

"Ah, to be young again," Paige said. She sat down on Rose's bed.

"You're not asleep, either. That argues for your own youth."

Paige shook her head ruefully. "There's no arguing away the difference between twenty-one and forty-one. The spirit is still willing but the flesh—oh, the flesh. It droops and wrinkles, and not all the remedies in all the ladies magazines can restore it. Enjoy your beauty while you may, Rose."

"I try not to be vain."

"It's not vanity; it's good sense. We enjoy the first strawberries of the season knowing how brief a time they last. Why not feel the same way about our beauty? I know I enjoyed being beautiful. When I was first a bride, that is."

"And the second time you were a bride?"

"Oh, I was a sober matron—for about fifteen minutes. I even wore a cap. Once."

"What happened to it?"

"Japhet threw it in the fire during breakfast." Aunt Paige laughed at the memory, her throat white in the candlelight. "He said he had married a dashing widow, not the matron of a girls' academy. It was a pretty thing, too. Valenciennes lace."

"I suggest you spare the cost of buying another. I doubt Sir Augustus will be any more forbearing."

"It's worth the cost for such a pretty compliment." As though she had only half heard Rose's comment, Paige sat up and darted a glance at her. "Sir Augustus won't have the opportunity, anyway. I have every intention of refusing him."

"Why on earth would you do anything so foolish?"

"My goodness, you are forthright. Has Augustus been talking to you?"

"Yes. He said you're afraid of losing another husband."

"I hadn't realized he was quite so perceptive." Paige smoothed the coverlet idly. "Marriage is a leap in the dark. Sir Augustus seems like a kindly, gentle, loving man, but how can I be sure? One has only to regard those unfortunate persons who are permanently tied to an uncongenial other to know how miserable such a marriage becomes."

"You can't seriously believe Sir Augustus will mistreat you. Why, he worships the ground you walk on."

"Now, perhaps. But what about later?"

"Shouldn't later take care of itself? I hate to think of you being alone for the rest of your life. What will you do if you don't marry again? You can't go to parties forever."

Paige laughed at her. "And they say there are no old heads on young shoulders. You sound like a grandmother counseling a giddy child."

"I'm sorry. I have no right to an opinion on such matters. What do I know? I've never even been . . . in love."

"Rose? What aren't you telling me?" Paige fixed her with a happily suspicious gaze.

"Nothing of consequence," Rose said, coloring, and told herself she wasn't lying. What could she tell her aunt? That she'd permitted a strange man to kiss her and that she'd never known so thrilling a moment before in her life? Could she say she had not the least notion of who he was and she cared even less? Was there any way to tell a dear relative one had completely lost one's mind, to the point where if the stranger asked her to, she'd elope with him without a second thought?

Rose realized all these things were true. It might not be love, but she knew no other name for this giddy feeling, which cast her high as the clouds one moment and lower than a dungeon floor the next.

"Do tell me if I'm to be confronted by some young man demanding your father's name and direction."

"If I have any warning, I'll share it with you."

"I've been meaning to ask you, my dearest, have

you quarreled with that large colonel? I haven't seen him in the throng lately."

"I think he's been ill," Rose said, remembering the way his eyes had seemed to burn like two coals.

"Too bad, though I should be grateful for my furniture's sake. Do you know the joints are weak in at least two of the drawing room chairs? I think it's the size of your admirers."

"I do have a few small ones," Rose said playfully. "The others just cast longer shadows."

"It's a small price to pay for your company. You know, you wouldn't worry about my being alone if I had some bright young creature about the house, would you?"

"No. Are you thinking of buying a dog?"

Paige laughed. "No, nor a cat. You've enjoyed London so much and I've enjoyed showing you all the sights. Would you consider making your home with me?"

"Permanently?" Rose forgot the questions that confused her in the light of this exciting development. "Oh, Aunt Paige, I hadn't even dreamed . . ."

"You would consider it, then? I know your mother might not like to spare you."

"Oh, I'm sure she'd have no objections . . . well, perhaps a few. She does like having me do those tasks that she finds too burdensome. The flowers, the accounts, interviewing the servants."

"Surely she could spare you for a few more months at least. I was becoming so boring living alone."

"All the more reason to marry Sir Augustus."

"You and he have persistence in common. I should send him to the right-about."

"Why don't you, then?"

"I am such a variable creature, Rose. I know I

should do what is right for the both of us, but it is so sweet to have a trifle of romance in one's life, especially when one is middle-aged. Seeing that twinkle in a man's eye is very cheering when all you see are wrinkles in the mirror. If only Augustus were willing to leave it at flirtation."

"He's serious."

"Yes." Paige shook her head sadly. "I know sending him away is the only right thing to do, yet I can think of a hundred reasons why I shouldn't do it just now. I'm afraid if I don't act quickly, I'll lose heart and never refuse him at all. We women are very good at convincing ourselves that wrong is right and the evidence of our minds is unimportant compared with the evidence of our hearts."

"Yes, we are good at that," Rose agreed dryly. "Well, Aunt Paige, you know my thoughts. I like Sir Augustus very much and can think of no one better suited to my dear aunt. Furthermore, I cannot bring myself to be so selfish as to desire to stay with you if it means crowding out your husband."

"Even if I did agree to marry him, I shouldn't do it until the close of the Season. You could still stay with me afterward. It wouldn't be as though Augustus and I were boy and girl, kissing furtively in corners."

"No, only openly on the terrace," Rose said, with a knowing glance.

Aunt Paige turned pink, a very flattering shade. "That is the problem," she said. "I can resist him by candlelight and by daylight, but moonlight destroys my resolves."

"I know what you mean," Rose said on a sigh.

Aunt Paige rose from the bed and drifted over to Rose. Giving her cheek a pat, she nodded knowingly. "Tell me when I shall be receiving the young man so

I may have your father's address already written out.
We mustn't lose any time."

"I will. You can enclose Sir Augustus's good wishes
to his future brother-in-law in the same cover."

"Minx," Paige said without rancor as she left the
room. She looked as if she would sleep now.

For Rose, however, sleep stayed frustratingly out of
reach. Every time she lay down, her thoughts would
begin to whirl around the events of the evening. The
worst was when she relived that breathtaking moment
when her unknown hero's head had blocked the
light, coming closer, while she, foolish virgin, didn't
resist. That was what sent her out of bed, unable to
bear her thoughts another moment.

For diversion, she knelt on the window seat and
pulled back her curtain. As she'd blown out her candle, she could see through the glass, instead of having
her own reflection meet her. Even at this hour, light
found its way into the garden. Every householder was
required by law to keep a lamp burning outside their
house, and some of it leaked into the rear of the
house, aided by a late-rising moon.

Rose unlatched her window and pushed it wide
open, past the sill. Distantly, she heard the heavy rumble of wheels over cobblestones as goods were
brought in for the early morning markets. It was so far
away, the rumble sounded like the sea.

In the garden, everything slept, even the rabbits that
lived in a corner by the wall, in defiance of cats, streets,
and Aunt Paige's once-a-week gardener. A little weak
perfume drifted up from the half-closed flowers, waiting for morning and the rising of their beloved sun.

Rose sighed and reached out to swing the window
closed. She paused, tensing. A sound, teasingly familiar, had reached her. Holding her breath, she listened

and it came again, the crunch of steps on gravel. They were much too loud to be a cat's.

Leaning forward, giving all her concentration to eyes and ears, she saw a form, no more than that, moving on the gravel path that led to Sir Niles's house, the same in every architectural detail to Aunt Paige's. The steps were not confident, striking out swiftly and unthinkingly. No, they wandered, two quick, several slower, several quicker again. These were the steps, Rose thought, of someone working out a problem, looking at it from all sides. A problem, say, like how to burglarize a house?

Though the intruder was too far away to be seen clearly in the uncertain light, Rose felt she could glimpse two articles of clothing. One, a cloak, judging by how hard it was to see details clearly. The other detail, half seen, half intuited when the unknown had turned his face to the moon, was a black something twisted across the eyes.

Without hesitation, as soon as Rose saw that, she threw on a pelisse and a pair of stout shoes. Just to be on the safe side, she pulled out a sturdy parasol. Thus attired, she paused by the window again, satisfied she could not be seen in her dark green coat any more than the Black Mask could be seen in his midnight-colored clothing.

The reassuring crunch of trodden gravel came again to her ears. Whoever was stalking around Sir Niles's garden at this hour was still there. She wondered if the Black Mask was planning to steal Sir Niles's collection of jewelry and gems.

Rose couldn't recall if she had ever been outside at night by herself. Even when she had been a child, growing up on the outskirts of a busy town, the outdoors was somewhere she went only with nurse or groom following behind. Even if she escaped these two guardians to go on some unauthorized escapade, Rupert went along.

If she had thought about it before she'd so impetuously hurried outside, she probably would have been nervous. But now that she was here, she felt oddly at home in the dark.

She noticed that, baffled by a high wall, the lights and sounds of a busy London night faded away into a low undercurrent, much less than it had appeared in her room. The lamplight was hardly more than a shimmer in the sky. From some bush nearby, a bird chirped in its sleep.

Rose advanced toward the white wall. By standing on tiptoe, she could just see over the top. "Hello?" she called softly. "Are you there?"

When the silence had stretched several minutes, Rose realized her position. There could be no explanation for her wandering around outside at night. A breath of air could only be achieved by an open window for a nice young lady. It was much too late for croquet, and the excuse of gardening by moonlight would work only for a sorceress. Besides, she'd obviously been mistaken in what she saw, or the visitor was long since gone. Yet why was her feeling of not being alone so strong?

Niles pressed his back against the wall, his breathing shallow, his mask fallen to the ground. He had never believed in a natural affinity of souls, but the suspicion had begun to sink in that Rose was linked to him in some way only metaphysics could explain.

What had possessed the girl to be awake now? Any other woman would be soundly sleeping after so strenuous an evening, not gazing out her window at nothing. Of course, he had every reason to believe Rose was no ordinary woman.

He heard her footsteps move off. Silently, he crept forward, walking along the grass verge on the edge of the gravel walk, seeking a soundless way to his own back door.

Some instinct or that affinity at work made him glance back just as the lever gave under his hand. A slight thud came to his ears as the top of a ladder seated itself against the top of the wall. He almost laughed aloud as he slipped inside the house. Were there no limits to Rose Spenser's intrepidity?

Only later did he realize he'd left his mask behind. Oh, well, he'd send Baxter out for it in the morning. Surely Rose hadn't dared to climb the wall and search. On the other hand . . .

Knowing now he'd find sleep unattainable until he checked, Niles sighed and put on his dressing gown. If she had climbed over, she'd find it impossible to climb back without help. Unlike Lady Marlton's gardener, his man didn't keep a ladder out where any passing young lady could find it. The walls that enclosed his garden had no exit save through the house, and even the usefully oblivious Baxter would notice if a young lady woke him up and asked him to show her out at four o'clock in the morning.

The only chivalrous thing would be to go to Miss Spenser's rescue. If she had found his mask, Niles would tell her the truth about his activities. Even as he made that vow, he recognized a feeling of disappointment. At some point, he'd begun to hope Rose would discover his secret for herself. If she came to him and declared she'd learned everything, he would confess and propose all in one breath. She might not want to marry Sir Niles, but could she resist the Black Mask?

For some reason, that notion didn't please him as much as it should have.

She stood about ten feet away from the wall, her hands on her hips defining her figure in a way that made Niles blink. "Trying to stare it down, Miss Spenser?"

Though she jumped, she did not, to her credit, squeak or scream. "You startled me," she said, "but then you always do." She went on glaring at the intransigent brick wall.

"I believe I shall omit the flurry of questions one usually asks when finding a young lady in one's garden in the predawn hours."

"My goodness, you really do have a formality for every occasion. The truth is, Sir Niles . . ."

He held up a finger. "In my experience, whenever anyone says 'the truth is,' they are working themselves up to tell a spectacular lie. Let us take whatever story you are intending to tell as read and permit me to help you return to your side of the garden wall."

"That would be most kind of you. But I have no intention of telling lies. I merely wished to ask you to help me."

"You aren't going to offer an explanation for your appearance here at so unusual an hour?"

"No. I don't believe it's any of your affair. Have you a ladder?"

"Not with me." Niles turned away to hide a grin. He attempted to summon up all his reserves of duty and every remembrance of his cold anger to stave off the impulse to drop to one knee and beg her to be his wife. He'd never imagined a woman like this when deciding to cling to his bachelorhood.

Falling in love right now showed a poor sense of timing, but Niles didn't care anymore. She'd found an unguarded path into his heart. Now that she had taken up residence there, Niles knew only gladness. He'd kept his anger hot for so long only to discover he could no longer summon it at will.

"Very well," he said, trying to keep his voice low and his attitude stuffy, when everything in him wanted to shout and dance. "I shall help you as though we were trying to seat you on your horse without a mounting block."

"Excellent. I'm very grateful."

Standing as close as she could to the wall, Rose lifted her skirt the necessary few inches to put her heel in his hand. A slight squeak escaped her lips as he lifted her with the clean jerk of pure athleticism. Her fingers scrabbled at the wall before they found a firm grip on the top.

She sat sideways on the wall, not unlike a lady in a saddle. There wasn't really a halo around her, but she made a light in his mind. He felt he could read her feelings by the set of her shoulders against the sky. She was puzzled as she looked down on him, her beautiful hair coming down from a bundle at the back.

"Thank you for not lecturing me," she said.

"I haven't the least shred of a right to. I hope I wouldn't even if I did have such a right."

"I don't believe you would. You deserve your title of 'the Most Polite Man in London,' though I would argue that 'most chivalrous' serves as well."

Niles bowed, trying not to laugh. "Always a pleasure to be of assistance."

"Do you mean that?"

"Of course. What further help do you require? If it

is something on your side of the wall, I'm afraid I shan't be much use, but I can try."

"No, not that. I can get down. I have a ladder."

"Excellent forethought. Then what may I do for you, Ro . . . Miss Spenser?"

"Ride with me today at seven. I have an appointment I do not wish to keep alone."

Niles tensed. "An appointment? Why not ask your brother to accompany you?"

"He'd try to stop me from keeping it, and I gave my word." When he didn't answer at once, busy with conjecture, she twitched her shoulders. "It's too much of an imposition. I'm sorry."

Niles caught her bare ankle to stop her swinging her feet over. "I shall be happy to serve you, Rose, in any capacity. I shall call for you at seven."

She held very still after the shock of his touch, but Niles could feel the fine trembling that shook her limb. "Not much sleep for us, then," she said with an attempt at lightness.

"I need very little sleep." He realized the impropriety of continuing to hold her by the leg, but his fingers seemed reluctant to let go. She had skin like silk shot with lightning, so smooth and yet vibrant.

"Good night," he said, releasing her and stepping back.

As she swung her legs over and felt for the first rung of the ladder with her feet, Rose's conscience pinched her with bony fingers. The mask she'd found on the ground nestled against her bosom. She should warn Sir Niles that the Black Mask had, most likely, already robbed him of his treasures.

Unless he planned to beguile the sleepless hours by

counting over his jewels, the odds were good he wouldn't discover his loss for some time. She hoped Rupert's vowels were stored in the same place so the Black Mask would have no trouble burglarizing Sir Niles's home a second time upon her instructions. She only hoped the Malikzadi would prove enough of a temptation not only to bring the Black Mask to her but to bribe him to carry out her plan.

Still and all, her plan would have difficult consequences for Sir Niles. She had every intention of paying back the debts at some future date, but Sir Niles's jewels would be gone forever. She tried to salve her conscience by reflecting that, if the Black Mask had already targeted the collection, Sir Niles's jewels were already as good as gone. It couldn't matter to him if Rupert's pledges disappeared as well.

Yet her better self would not be silenced by such specious reasoning. Sir Niles had been kind again, true, but even if he'd been a beast to her, as he'd been to poor Colonel Wapton, didn't she owe it to him to inform him a burglar might try to steal from him? Perhaps he would try to protect his jewel collection. The Black Mask could no doubt overwhelm any such effort as easily as snapping his fingers.

Only after Rose had again retired to her room, slipping silently through the sleeping house, did another issue arise to torment her.

She had only an absent smile for Mr. Quayle's groom walking her mare from around the corner. When Sir Niles arrived promptly at seven, Rose asked him the question that had troubled her—as soon as a thrilled Aunt Paige pulled her head in after waving to Sir Niles.

"After last night," she began as the horses ambled toward the park, "am I compromised?"

Sir Niles suffered a sudden fit of coughing. "Comp . . . compromised?"

"Yes. I was out very late, and you were wearing a dressing gown. Someone with a suspicious mind might wonder what we were doing and why you were helping me return over the wall."

"Fortunately, there was no one to see."

"I hope there wasn't," Rose murmured, her color high. The Black Mask might have seen them.

"Is over the wall the only way out of your back garden?" she asked.

"Yes, except through the house. It's the usual way for houses of that vintage. They didn't want the less fortunate setting up housekeeping in the garden shed."

Rose frowned perplexedly. How then had the Black Mask entered the garden? She might have thought she'd dreamed seeing him if it weren't for the mask tucked away in her stockings drawer.

"Then you feel my reputation is quite secure?" Rose asked, returning to her previous preoccupation.

"Entirely. If I thought otherwise, I would be requesting permission to call on your father."

"I see. Yes, that's very clear."

Sir Niles leaned forward to catch the cheek branch of her mare's bit. Obediently, the mare stopped. "Miss Spenser, kindly don't misconstrue. That is by no means the only circumstance which would prompt me to such an action. Indeed, I . . ."

Until the whip cracked in the air, neither of them realized that they'd brought their horses to a stop in the middle of the street. A heavily laden dray swerved past them, the driver's shout singeing the air, while several other drivers, slower and more careful, made vivid comments on the absentmindedness of the gentry.

When they reached the other side of the thoroughfare, Sir Niles had evidently thought the better of what he'd intended to say. "A very pleasant day for a ride. Where is your 'appointment' to be found?"

"Down the main path, where the bushes grow thickest."

"Is that wise? Notice I ask no other questions."

"I appreciate it very much." Rose reminded herself Sir Niles had promised not to demand explanations. Perversely, she felt all the more compelled to explain. "I don't want you to misunderstand. I'm not meeting a clandestine lover or anything like that. It's merely that Colonel Wapton asked me to meet him here this morning."

"Colonel Wapton? Am I not a strange choice to accompany you, then? You did not approve of my attitude toward him the other day."

"That's why I asked you," Rose confessed. "I'm not frightened of him, but he looked and acted so oddly yesterday. I know if anything's amiss, you'll know what to do."

"You saw him yesterday?"

She told him about how Wapton had appeared from the underbrush like a highwayman. Glancing at him, Rose could hardly believe the way the tension made his jaw look so strong. For one instant, she felt as though she rode beside a stranger.

"I shall wait for you a few yards away," he said. "I shan't overhear any confidences the colonel chooses to make, but if necessary, I can be at your side in an instant." As an obvious afterthought, he added, "Will that be satisfactory?"

"Entirely. We are all but there now."

Rose had worn her very nicest riding habit, all blue broadcloth and silver basketwork buttons like a man's coat. A long white veil twisted around the glossy blackness of her hat, floating behind her on the breeze stirred up by her passing. She had not worn it for the colonel. As she reached the rendezvous, she looked back toward Sir Niles and gave her riding crop a slight flick like a salute. He rose up in his stirrups and she smiled.

When she looked around again, Colonel Wapton stood before her. If he'd been unkempt yesterday, today he looked all but slovenly. His eyes were red and even more sunken in a face that looked more like a skull.

"You're unwell," she said, concerned.

"It doesn't matter. Who's that? Rupert?" He squinted down the path.

"Just a friend," Rose said, suddenly wishing she'd asked anyone in the world to accompany her besides Sir Niles. What could it look like to the colonel but that she preferred the man who had all but thrown him from her aunt's home? With a shock, Rose realized she did indeed prefer Sir Niles and always had. "You asked me to come here, sir. You had a favor to ask, I think?"

From under his coat, the colonel produced a flat leather satchel, the buckle and tongue cinched as tightly as possible. "Keep this for me. Just for a few days."

"I?" She took it from his hand because he seemed so insistent. "Haven't you a bank or a lawyer? My father says there's nothing more secure than a bank."

"I don't trust anyone." His gaze flicked constantly from Rose to the distant man on horseback. He even turned on his heel once to scan the bushes. "But no one would suspect you of keeping my secrets."

"I'm not sure I wish to keep them. Take this back again, if you please."

"It will only be for a few days. A few . . . When it's safe, yes, when it's safe, I'll come for them. I . . ." He pushed his hand through his greasy hair. She noticed how it shook with fear or grief, and pity touched her.

"Surely, sir, whatever is amiss, someone at your regiment can help you."

"My regiment," he whispered. Suddenly, horribly, tears glistened in his bloodshot eyes. "My regiment. No, the last place . . . besides," he added with a whiplash change of mood, "I don't trust anyone there. No, I don't trust anyone."

Colonel Wapton glanced up at her, and the intensity of his gaze was like sunlight focused through a magnifying lens. "Keep it safe. Tell no one you have it. Do this for me, for one who admired you."

"I will keep it because you are an officer in His Majesty's Service," she said. He winced as though she'd raised her riding crop to strike him. Puzzled and pained, Rose continued, "But pray come to retrieve this parcel as soon as you may. I don't wish to keep it any longer than the few days you have promised."

"If I don't come for it in three days, you may destroy the contents. It won't matter then." More composed, he glanced again toward the figure on horseback down the path. Rose turned her head as well. Sir Niles sat like a statue, his horse under perfect control. When she brought her gaze back to the path beside her, the colonel had disappeared. Only the faintly waving branches of the bush beside her showed which way he'd gone.

Twelve

"Men," said Rose with newfound conviction, "are more confusing than French verbs."

Aunt Paige looked up from her petit-point work. "What prompts this grand statement?" she asked with a girlish smile.

"Sir Niles. You saw him when we left. Wasn't he in a cheerful mood?"

"So far as I could tell from the window, yes."

Rose flung her beautiful hat onto an empty chair. "Would you believe he hardly spoke three words to me after . . . after we reached the park?"

"That doesn't sound like Sir Niles. He's usually so courteous, even to excess."

"Not today. I know it's difficult to converse on horseback, but it isn't impossible. Yet every to every gambit I tried, he would return nothing but single word answers. Not always the right word, either!"

"Perhaps he was preoccupied by something, business affairs or such like. All the same, he is usually more attentive, especially, or so I have noticed, to you."

"Yes," Rose admitted. "I thought so, too. Now I can see my mistake."

"I thought you didn't care for him. Isn't he the most cold and unfeeling of men?"

"Yes, he is every bit of that. Even so, I thought, sometimes, that he treated me differently from other women."

Paige made room for Rose to sit beside her. "Search your heart, Rose. Have you ever liked a man more than Sir Niles?"

Rose thought of a kiss freely given to a man of mystery whose face she could not see. It was a thrill that would live in her memory for as long as she had breath. And yet . . .

"Sir Niles isn't as cold and harsh as I first believed," Rose admitted softly. "He has, on several occasions, shown me amazing consideration." She remembered the kindness of his eyes, how they laughed when she amused him, giving her such a sensation of triumph, and how intensely they dwelled on her when she longed for his understanding.

"On the other hand," Rose went on, interrupting Paige before she could begin the words she'd opened her mouth to say, "he is terribly moody. I have seen him change within the space of a minute between charming, kind, all I could wish, to someone whose lightest word can chill my blood."

"People do have moods, Rose. I have them myself."

"Not like this. There's no reason for these lightning changes. If there were, even if I couldn't completely understand his reasons, perhaps then I would fall in love with him."

"Oh, my dear . . ." Paige said, her eyes wide. "You couldn't try a little harder, could you? He'd be exactly the right sort of husband for you. He's so generous, and the Alardyce fortune is more than sufficient to command the elegances of life. You'd never know a moment's want or worry."

"Not financially, I suppose. As it is, however, I could

never trust myself to such a man. I should be too afraid."

"You might change him once you were married," Paige ventured.

"And if I couldn't? What then? I couldn't live on the edge of a volcano."

"If he loved you enough . . ."

"If he loved me, wouldn't I know it by now? Who is it who said 'love and a cough cannot be hidden'?"

Paige reflected a moment. "I think you are failing to account for Sir Niles's reputation. He has so often shown disdain for marriage. Were he to propose to you, he would have to face a great deal of talk. Anyone would shrink at first from such a step."

"He's no coward."

Even in the midst of her preoccupation, Rose noticed Aunt Paige frowned at her response.

"It's not cowardice," she said, her voice rising. "We live in this world of gossip and social rivalry. It may not be an ideal world, but it is ours and we understand the rules by which it is governed. One cannot simply throw all that away without some due thought toward what a different life would mean. How is Sir Niles to build himself a new place in that world as a married man? I can't see him giving up London society to be a gentleman farmer or a banker, can you?"

"But if you are in love," Rose said, "as you obviously love the general . . ."

"Love isn't everything when you are middle-aged as it is when you are young."

"So you have said."

The silence between them hummed with reconsidered arguments. Paige spoke first. "Have you considered that if you were to marry Sir Niles, Rupert's debts would vanish? Sir Niles couldn't press his brother-in-law for payment. Furthermore, the only thing that prevents Rupert from joining the army is your father's adamant refusal to purchase a commission. Sir Niles could purchase any number of them and never miss the cost."

"I am not likely to marry for the sole purpose of providing my brother with a commission. There are better reasons."

Rose decided that, if she could not be honest about everything to everyone, she could at least tell the unvarnished truth to her favorite female relation. "I love you dearly, Aunt Paige. I could wish my mother entered into my affairs with even half your sympathy and affection. But I must tell you without roundaboutation that if you don't marry Sir Augustus O'Banyon and embrace the happiness he can give you, I will think of you as nothing more than a fool."

"Rose!" Paige shrank away in shock. "This to me?"

"Have you any reason to doubt his affections, except the speed with which he declared them? No, you have not. Do you know of anything against his character? Surely someone among your gossiping friends would have informed you had he a wife secreted somewhere, or if he'd given any cause for disquiet to the army."

"No, I've heard nothing."

"Then what else holds you back but fear of the unknown?"

"The same thing, in short, that holds you back from Sir Niles," Paige shot back.

Rose held up her hands, acknowledging a hit. "With one difference, Aunt. Sir Augustus has given you every evidence of affection including, as I believe you told me, a formal proposal of marriage. Sir Niles has not demonstrated a single such sign." Yet even as she spoke, her ankle tingled as she remembered his firm, warm touch encircling her skin.

She ignored it. A tingling ankle, much like a stolen kiss at a ball, was nothing to base one's future life upon. Rational and unbiased thinking would give her a firmer foundation for wedded happiness.

"Are you certain he has not made any such advance? His partiality for your company has been noticed even by less interested parties than your aunt."

"He has never said or done anything even the strictest moralist could take exception to."

Again, Paige laughed. "Shall I commiserate with you?"

Rose smiled shyly. She had sounded rather forlorn. "I have always been too diffident to encourage him. Not to mention, what would I do if he laughed at me?"

In her room, Rose picked up the leather satchel which Hurst had carried up for her. Though prey to the gnawing tooth of curiosity, Rose knew it would be against her honor to peek at whatever it was Colonel Wapton went to such lengths to conceal. He'd not given her permission to look inside.

Somewhat cavalierly, she tossed the satchel into the wardrobe and shut the door upon it.

Having had no sleep the night before, Rose had told Paige she was intending to rest for the remainder of the day and meant to take her noon meal in bed. As she undressed, she had cause to open the wardrobe several times to remove her nightdress and robe, to choose the clothes she would wear later, and to retrieve a chemise that had fallen down inside. Every time she opened the door, she fought with herself again over whether she should undo the clasp and look inside the leather case.

Her better self prevailed, but her baser nature wouldn't let the matter go.

When her maid came up, Rose hailed her with relief. "I've made rather a mess," she said, watching Lucy pick up her habit and underclothing.

"Never you mind, miss. I'll have the horse hairs off this in a brace o' shakes. Coo, you did look a picture riding off with Sir Niles. He's ever so handsome."

"Did you see us?" Rose asked.

"Oh, yes, miss. Me 'n' Cook was watching from the area window. If you stand on a chair and kind of peer to the left, you can see the street plain as plain. Ever so useful when you want to know how many to serve during morning calls." Lucy cast a glance around the bedroom. "I'll come for your boots when I bring up your nuncheon, miss. Her laidyship said how you'd want to take a bit of a rest this morning."

"Yes, I'm very sleepy. It's not too much trouble to bring me a tray?"

"No trouble, miss. But you'll be wanting to get up later, no doubt. You're going to the Duchess of Kent's cotillion ball tonight, aren't you?"

"Yes, after the opera," Rose said and sighed. She felt all the more tired just thinking about another night on her feet.

"That's what I told Baxter. Coo, he's a one, he is. Looks like a piece of string dipped in tallow. No more flesh on him than on a stick. But he's a jolly one—always laughin' and crackin' jokes. Wonder how he keeps a straight face when he's talking to his master."

"Baxter? Who's he?"

"That Sir Niles's valet. Valet? To hear him tell it, he runs the whole house."

Rose sat up slowly, plumping the pillows behind

her. "Sir Niles's man wanted to know if I'd be at the cotillion tonight?"

"Yes, miss. I didn't do wrong to tell him? He said you'd mentioned it to his master, but Sir Niles is that absentminded he forgot what you'd said. It's all right?"

"Yes, Lucy. Quite all right. Wake me at one, please."

"A pleasure, miss." She went out, her arms full of broadcloth and linen.

Why did Sir Niles want to know where she'd be tonight? Fresh from her conversation with Paige, Rose worried that maybe she was right. What if Sir Niles were planning some kind of proposal? At first, she dismissed the idea. Nothing prevented him from coming here and making his intentions known in the proper style. Sir Niles would never do anything so gauche as propose marriage at a ball.

A little while later, sleepily, she wondered if Paige could be right. If so, might not overwhelming passion drive Sir Niles into making a public declaration of his feelings? In that unlikely event, how would she respond?

Rose's eyes closed as she sketched out a delightful scene in which Sir Niles halted in the very steps of a waltz to ask her to be his forever. As is the case in dreams, she could waltz perfectly, revolving in Sir Niles's arms as the music played faster and faster. She fell asleep while still trying to determine whether it would be more enjoyable to accept him then and there or to turn him down and show the world how little she thought of him.

Sadly, neither scenario could come true without Sir Niles. He was nowhere to be found. Rose spent so much time scanning the opera house that she hardly watched the opera, barely noticing when the taller soprano pushed the smaller one into the orchestra pit. During the interval, only Rose's social training kept her from being rude to several of Aunt Paige's oldest friends.

"Sir Augustus can't abide the opera," Paige said as they resumed their seats. "A pity, when I love it so."

"Is he meeting you later?" Rose asked.

"I haven't the least notion. He never sent me so much as a line scribbled on the back of a card."

"Men," Rose said with a tiny sniff.

"Indeed." Paige plied her fan a bit too rapidly. "Speaking of whom, wasn't Rupert supposed to accompany us this evening?"

"He probably had another engagement," Rose said, not thinking of her brother. "Or some good chap named Blank or Dash gave him a tip about a sure bet and he hurried off to waste his money."

Three hours later at the cotillion, Rose stopped by her aunt's chair and waited, smiling stiffly, until Paige looked up inquiringly. "This is the dullest party I've ever been to," Rose said, hardly moving her lips. "Shall we go?"

"Considering that your dance card has been filled since the moment we arrived, I wouldn't think you could be bored."

"I am, though. Everyone's talking, but no one's saying anything I wish to hear."

"You are too severe." Paige lifted one shoulder in defeat. "It's just as well. I've had a headache for the last hour from smelling the candles."

"Sir Augustus never arrived?" Rose asked as they waited for their cloaks.

"No," Paige said, pouting like a schoolgirl. "Sir Niles?"

"No, and I don't care either."

When they reached the house, Hurst met them at the door as usual. "If I may have a word, my lady?"

Though his carefully cultivated expression of bland efficiency was unimpaired, his voice was less perfectly controlled. Furthermore, when he turned toward the light to follow Paige into the drawing room, they saw a large rapidly purpling bruise on his forehead.

"Hurst!" Paige exclaimed. "Are you hurt? Sit down, man."

"Thank you, my lady. I confess I feel somewhat shaken."

"Shall I pour you some brandy?" Rose asked. The butler had been very kind to both her and her brother during their visit.

"No, miss. I took the liberty earlier." He straightened his posture despite being seated and looked his mistress directly in the eye. "I regret to tell you we discovered a burglary, my lady."

"A burglary?" Paige exchanged an astonished glance with Rose. "Good heavens, my jewels!"

Excitement began to bubble in Rose's blood. "What was stolen, Hurst?"

"Nothing, miss."

Aunt Paige sat down with a thump. "Nothing?"

"We apprehended something was amiss before the culprit breached the house, my lady. The tweeny, while taking far too long to finish the dishes, glimpsed a mysterious personage slinking through the garden. By the time it occurred to her to inform the cook, the miscreant had opened one of the windows. We believe he was alarmed by the cook's screams and beat a retreat. We found a small crust of mud on the runner in the hall."

"So he did enter the house! How can you be certain nothing was stolen?"

"I took the liberty of instructing your maid to take an inventory of all your jewels."

Rose gasped and turned it deftly into a cough. Aunt Paige was too distracted to notice, but Rose thought Hurst gave her a calculating glance.

"I myself counted the silver. Not a single piece is missing. It is my belief the thief did not penetrate any farther into the house than the lower hall."

"But the bruise on your forehead," Aunt Paige said.

He felt the mark gingerly. "The cook suffered an attack of hysteria, my lady, and seemed to suspect me of being a housebreaker in disguise."

"Oh, dear," Aunt Paige said. "I hope you were able to reassure her."

"Regrettably, my lady, I was not. She has intimated her intention to quit your service this very night."

This was a greater calamity than an army of looters. "I had better have a word with her."

"Indeed, my lady." He hefted himself to his feet as she hurried out.

"I'm surprised my brother didn't help you. Or wasn't he at home, Hurst?"

"Yes, miss. But he heard nothing. I didn't wish to disturb him in order to receive his instructions, and believe it would not have availed anyway." A glint in the otherwise impassive man's eye told Rose volumes.

"Is he very much the worse for drink?"

"Yes, miss."

"Very well. I'll not trouble him, either, though he'll be miserable that he missed all the excitement."

Hurst cleared his throat as she went to the door. "If I may . . . another word, miss."

"Yes, Hurst? You should lie down; I feel certain you have a headache."

"Indeed I have, miss." He reached into his pocket and brought out a somewhat crumpled piece of paper.

Rose colored as the butler smoothed the paper between his hands. "Lucy found this in your jewel box."

Taking the paper from him, Rose saw that the monogrammed wafer on the back was still stuck down fast, quite undisturbed. "I can explain . . ." she began.

The mark on his brow in no way detracted from the butler's tremendous natural dignity. He held up one hand. "Explanations are unnecessary. However, should you wish to contact the Black Mask again, please do so outside the house. Thank you."

"Thank you. I doubt I will have cause."

The butler defrosted. "Lucy won't say anything about your message, miss. Neither will I."

"Girlish folly, Mr. Hurst, that's all."

In her room, she undressed for bed in a bitter mood. It seemed as though her one chance to achieve contact with the Black Mask had failed due to a tweeny's procrastination. She'd built her hopes too high that the Black Mask would attempt to steal the Malikzadi. She knew, however, her disappointment stemmed more from his trying to steal it while she was not at home. She'd hoped to see him again to discover not only if he'd steal back Rupert's vowels from Sir Niles but also to learn if he'd stolen a kiss from her.

Setting her mind firmly, even grimly, on sleep, Rose tucked her hands under her cheek. She heard the clock strike the quarter hour, but not the half.

What woke her, however, was not the clock. When she'd first come to town, every time she entered her bedroom, she would step on a single loose board. Soon she avoided it without thought. Now, in the midst of a dream, she heard the strange creaky rattle of that loose board. Pushing herself up on her elbow, she blinked into the darkness. "Lucy? Aunt Paige?"

She reached out to uncover the shaded candle on her bedside table.

Thirteen

Suddenly sleep fled. "Oh, it's you," she said.

The black-clad man in her room froze. Perhaps he'd never heard such a soft, welcoming tone from any of his other victims.

"I wish you hadn't woken up," he said. "I swear I'm thinking this crib is cursed. I never had such trouble in my life." His hoarse voice definitely had a tinge of the lower orders, though an occasional flourish of language showed he had ambition above his station.

"There's a loose board in the floor near the door," Rose told him. "I couldn't help waking up."

"Well, that's your bad luck."

"Bad luck? No, I'm pleased. I want to talk to you."

"Talk to me? You should be screaming the place down 'round my ears."

He dressed all in black, just as all the masqueraders had surmised. Like her mysterious masked man, he wore riding breeches and unpolished boots. For the rest, his black shirt hung loose, open at the throat. Over his mouth and jaw, he'd wound a black muffler. His eyes gleamed like burning onyx between the muffler and the brim of his hat, pulled low over his brow.

As she lay there on her side, even though the coverlet was pulled up under her arms, Rose saw a greater fire come into his eyes. "T-turn around," she said. "If you please."

"Why should I?"

"So I may put on my dressing gown. It's ridiculous trying to carry on a conversation like this."

"I like it," he said. How could she tell he wore a grin when his lower face was hidden? Nevertheless, a grin had come into his tone.

"I said, *If you please.*"

He twitched his shoulders in what might have been a shrug, but he turned his face away.

"Not there," Rose hastened to add. "There's a mirror in that corner."

"I'll cover my eyes then, eh? While you sneak up behind me and hit me over the head with the vase? No, thanks; I've had some o' that before now."

"I promise I'm only going to put on something decent."

Hastily, she threw on the regrettably plain wrapper. It was all wrong for a girl doing a dashing and daring thing like entertaining a notorious criminal in her bedroom. She wished she had one like Aunt Paige's, all but transparent lawn covered with lavish amounts of lace. But all she had was cashmere in a sad color with brown net trimming she'd made herself last winter. Made to fasten up to her throat, one could praise it for being warm, practical, and hard-wearing, but it was far from alluring.

"Where's your jewel case?" he asked, facing the wall.

"It's not here," Rose lied. "After your earlier attempt to break in, the butler moved everything. I don't know where he's hidden it." She only wished she'd thought of it, but never suspected he might try twice on the same night.

"A pity. Is it safe?"

"Safe?"

"To turn around."

"Oh, yes, I'm sorry."

He turned and looked her over in a way that made the cashmere feel as sheer as lawn. He even looked at her bare feet, which shrank back behind the folds of fabric like snails retreating into their shells. "Charming," he said, starting to cough again.

"Are you quite well?" she asked, coming around the foot of the bed. "You shouldn't be out in the night air if you have a cough."

"Don't worry about me," he said, his voice roughening again. "You said you wanted to talk to me. Make it quick. I can't stay; it's too dangerous."

"How did you break in a second time?" Rose asked. "I felt sure Hurst would lock up with special care."

"He did. But on my first visit tonight I fixed the window so it looked to lock but wouldn't."

"Clever-clocks," Rose said in admiration. "Is that how you managed to rob all those other people?"

"Now what do you take me for? Doing 'em all the same way'd get me in trouble quick as winking. All them genu'y'd be having fits if they ever figured how I done 'em. These fancy houses is easier'n nuts to crack."

"I can think of one house you couldn't possibly . . . er . . . crack."

"T'ain't no such place in all the world," the Black Mask said, his King's English eroding from moment to moment.

"You mean you've found a way to rob Sir Niles Alardyce?"

"Sir Niles . . ." He coughed again, more lengthily, and Rose came closer yet.

"When you go home, make yourself a nice cup of tea. Put honey in it, if you have any."

"I can always steal some from the kitchen on m'way out. Now, look here, miss."

"I'm Rose Spenser. How d'you do?"

"How d' . . . now look here." He backed away. "M'cough and my business is me own concern. I don't know nothin' about some bloody Sir Dandy."

"You were in his garden last night. Weren't you deciding how to . . . oh, were you observing this house?"

"'At's right."

"Oh, but you really should consider Sir Niles's home. He's quite a famous connoisseur of rare gems."

"Him? I heard of him. Terrible great traps all over his house and him? Deadly, they say, with any sort of weapon. Pistols, arrows, knives . . . it's all one to him."

"I think you have the wrong man in mind," Rose said. "Sir Niles may be all you say regarding his prowess with weapons." Remembering the strength of the man who'd lifted her onto a high garden wall without so much as a grunt of effort, Rose added, "He's very strong as well. But he'd never spoil his decor with any kind of trap. They say, however, his collection of jewelry belonging to former royal houses is second to none."

"Royal stuff, eh?"

"Yes. They say he possesses several pieces that belonged to the late queen of France."

"Who's that then? That Josephine what married the little Frenchie?"

"No. Marie Antoinette, of course. She had wonderful taste in expensive baubles. Though I have heard Sir Niles also has some earrings that belonged to the Empress Josephine as well. Someone told me she'd staked some large ruby earrings in a card game without telling her husband and Sir Niles bought them later from the winner's widow."

"Hmph. Paste, most likely. Some little old woman

pitched me a story like that once. Claimed what she was selling were some Russian empress's own bracelets. Turned out the Empress of Russia liked chips of glass and the sort of brass what turns in five minutes and leaves your arm green for a month."

"I'm sure nothing like that would happen. Sir Niles is very knowledgeable about jewels. It would be foolish to make any attempt to sell him a fraud."

"Them's the ones what's usually easiest to fool. The more a flat thinks he knows about one thing, the less he knows about the rest of the world. Someone like that can be fooled, easy as winking."

"You wouldn't say so if you knew Sir Niles as I do. Listen, if you could enter Sir Niles's house, could you find his hiding place?"

"Could be anywhere. Wait, here. Why you so keen on having me break into this gentry's house? What's he ever done to you?"

"Nothing to me. He holds some few of my brother's IOUs."

"For which he finds himself unable to raise the wind?" He gave a short bark of laughter.

"Exactly. If you could, while abstracting Sir Niles's treasures, bring me those IOUs."

"Hardly a problem." He coughed more violently than ever. "What's in this for the one's that taking all the risk?"

"Perhaps I should postpone my plan until you are feeling better. Unless you know someone who'd be willing to take on a small job for large rewards."

"Yeah. Me. So what's in it for me, then?"

"You take the jewels and bring me the IOU chits. In exchange, I will give you all my jewelry, a large crystal sphere that I bought at the Burlington Exchange, and the Malikzadi."

"The what?"

"It's a ruby, very large, very beautiful."

"Where is it?" he said, running his eyes over her again.

"In my jewel case, as I told you. Tomorrow, however, once the alarmed servants are reassured, I will ask for my case to be returned to me, as it should have been tonight. Bring me my brother's debts, and you shall have it all."

"Just walk back in this cursed crib again?"

"You're not afraid, are you?"

He straightened up, almost to a military point of correctness. "I'm not afraid of nothing. All right. I'll do it. But I get to keep everything I find but them bits of paper."

"That's right," Rose said and sighed in relief. She'd thought he was going to refuse. "Can you read?"

"Tolerable, missus." He would have tugged at his forelock, Rose thought, if it hadn't been for the muffler around his neck starting to unwind.

"Just look for the name Rupert Spenser on each one and bring me all those you find. Can you be discreet? I don't want Sir Niles to know you were searching for the vowels."

"He won't know nothing 'til he goes to the cupboard and finds it swept clean."

"Good. I don't want any violence." She crossed the room to the big wardrobe. "I'll leave the details up to you, shall I?"

"I am the professional," he said with pride.

"Oh, by the way . . ." She opened the wardrobe door, pushing the satchel back in with her foot when it started to fall out. Taking down a homemade reticule she'd decided was too provincial for London, she reached inside. "I found your mask by the wall yesterday night. Do be more careful."

This time when he turned away from her, he cared much more about what could be seen in a mirror. "I missed it," he said. When he spun around again, Rose took a hard look at him, now that she could see his mouth and chin. He could be . . . then again, the man who had kissed her hadn't seemed uneducated. Something about his voice . . .

"Have we met before?" he asked, before the words in her mouth could be spoken.

"I don't believe so," Rose said politely. "It's hard to tell with the mask. Are you a member of Parliament?"

"No, I don't hold with robbery on that scale." He touched the nosepiece of the stiffened leather mask as if to be certain it had not slipped down. "Can I ask you a question, miss?"

"Certainly," Rose said, not without reservations.

"If you want these bits of paper back so bad, why don't you just ask this Sir Niles gentry for 'em? Seems to me a pretty gel like yourself ought to have him wound 'bout your little finger."

"Sir Niles belongs to a class of men that treat IOUs very seriously. I would rather have them disappear than continue to blight a young man's happiness. Rest assured, however, that as soon as I can contrive some method, my brother will repay every cent. He'll be going into the bank soon and will be paid a regular salary."

"They tried that with me once, putting me into harness when I wanted to run free. Didn't work. Don't suppose your brother'd consider becoming my apprentice? Hours aren't so good, but the money keeps rolling in."

"Until you wind up twisting in the wind," Rose said and saw him jump as if stung.

"What d'you want to go and say that for? Ain't this house cursed enough without you dragging in a gibbet?"

"Ssh." Rose held her finger to her lips, shutting her eyes to focus on the tiny sound she'd heard. "Please keep your voice down," she said, demonstrating.

The Black Mask came so close, she could smell the leather of his mask. Surprisingly, he himself did not have any offensive odor, only a clean scent she couldn't place. She hadn't smelled it in her mysterious man's embrace, which convinced her more than ever that some buck was merely entertaining himself last night.

"You can say what you like," he murmured, his voice hoarser still with the effort of whispering. "This Alardyce beau must be a mean-spirited fellow if you'd rather trust me than him."

"I told you why . . . besides, my brother wouldn't like it."

"He would like you cavorting with the criminal classes?"

"No, of course not." He stood much too close, but Rose found herself with no more space for retreat behind her. "I just want him to be happy."

"What about you?" His breath teased her cheek, and it, too, held no trace of vileness.

Slightly off balance, Rose caught at his forearm to steady herself. It was like catching an iron bar. "I want to be happy, too."

His fingertips were surprisingly smooth and gentle as he ran them lightly over her cheek. Rose's eyes swept closed as she involuntarily concentrated on the sensations he aroused. "Keep your rings and such," he said, his lips touching her ear. "I'll claim my own reward."

He stepped back. "Look out in the hall to see if the house is stirring."

Feeling as if she'd escaped her fate by a hair's breadth, Rose looked and listened with her door open a crack. "I think it's all clear," she said.

"I'll go the way I came." He swept past her into the darkened hall. "Go back to bed." His voice was less than a whisper, and she couldn't be sure she hadn't heard him add a very rude word.

In the morning, her rational nature told her it had all been a dream. The Black Mask could not have stood in her bedroom and talked to her. It was just too impossible to believe.

Even as she went to the wardrobe to take down the reticule, she told herself how foolish she was to bother checking for the mask. It hadn't gone anywhere, for there'd been no one to take it.

Pulling open the drawstring, she plunged in her hand. Only the cardboard bottom met her questing fingers. Opening the bag fully, she upended it and shook.

Rose thought at first she'd merely moved the mask and then forgotten she'd done it. Or perhaps she'd walked in her sleep. She'd heard of people doing all sorts of strange things while sleepwalking—painting pictures, picking flowers, even untying knots they'd tied while awake.

Despite resisting the notion with logic and good sense, she gave in to the impact of reality. Though she'd not been embarrassed with the Black Mask in the room—why not?—in hindsight, she was one entire blush. If meeting Sir Niles under perfectly innocent circumstances in the garden put her reputation in jeopardy, how much more shameful to meet a famous criminal in her bedroom.

Suddenly, being alone did not appeal to her. She threw on her dressing gown, pulling the softness up to her throat. Hurrying down the hallway, she rapped sharply on Rupert's door. When he did not immediately answer, she rapped again, harder, her other hand on the doorknob.

It ripped through her grasp as Rupert yanked the door open. He raised one hand to shield his eyes against the dim light of the hall. He wore his breeches and a stained shirt. His cheeks and chin were covered with bristles and his lips were cracked, a white crust around them. His breath smelled like a mad alchemist's workshop.

"Rupert!" Rose, shocked by his appearance, shrank back.

"What the devil? Rose, what do you want?"

"I . . . I need to talk to you."

"Now? Can't it wait? I have the devil's own headache."

"You were drinking?"

He gave a hollow laugh. "Who? Me?"

Rose hesitated before asking her next question, but she needed to know. "Did you . . . gamble? Very much?"

He shrugged and rubbed his forehead. "I don't know. Maybe. For the love of heaven, Rose, would you ask someone to bring me some coffee? I don't know where my man has wandered off to."

"Yes, of course," Rose said, moved to pity. "But if you could just tell me . . ."

"I told you, I don't know," he snarled. "Why are you bothering me about that? It's none of your business."

"I can't bear to watch you destroying yourself. At this rate, what will be left for the army?"

"What difference can it make? I'll never have the money to join."

"Not if you keep gambling."

"How else am I to get it? If my luck weren't so cursed bad . . ."

"If . . . if I could find the money for you . . ."

As if he were a prisoner shown an open window which led to either freedom or death, wild hope and tormenting doubt battled across Rupert's dissipated countenance. "How could you?"

"I might marry a wealthy man. A brother-in-law could buy you a commission. Father couldn't stop you then, as you are of age. He'd have to accept a *fait accompli.*"

"Who? Who wants to marry you?"

"How much do you owe?"

"What? You can't be planning to marry someone depending on how much I owe? No, Rose. I'm not worth that."

He stumbled forward and wrapped an arm around her shoulders, giving her a rough, brotherly hug. "You just forget all about me. I'll go to perdition in my own way. But don't you go making a sacrifice of yourself. Anything would be better than that."

Rose blinked back tears. "No, no, Rupert. It's going to be all right."

A giggle interrupted them. When they looked around, Lucy, pretty in her mobcap, dipped them a curtsy. "Begging your pardon, Miss Rose, Mr. Rupert. Her ladyship asks if you'd lower your voices to consider the hour."

Rose stepped out of Rupert's encircling arms. "Lucy, would you bring my brother some coffee?" She rolled her eyes at him drolly. "And could you arrange for a bath?"

"For you, miss?" Lucy's dimples showed.

"No. For Mr. Spenser."

Rupert glanced between the two grinning girls. "Why do I feel as though you are trying to drop me a hint? Kindly don't spare my feelings."

"Very well, then. Rupert, dearly as I love you, I must tell you . . ."

"Never mind, never mind. Lucy, coffee first. Pots of it."

"Yes, sir."

When Lucy came to take down Rose's breakfast tray, she was no longer smiling. "There's a dreadful row going on downstairs, miss," she replied when Rose asked her what was wrong.

"Row? The cook isn't quarreling with Hurst, is she?"

"No, miss. It's her ladyship. She and the general are having the most dreadful row. We're that worried, miss."

Rose had only to slip on her shoes to be dressed. "Should I go down?"

"Would you? It's not right, so loving as they mostly are."

Rose tied her shoelaces, reflecting that the question of whether the servants knew of Aunt Paige's romance had been answered. Although judging by the raised voices that met her at the bottom of the stair, the question of romance might not need answering soon.

"You're being so unreasonable," Aunt Paige said, in the tone of a woman pushed to the limits of patience.

"And you're as stubborn as Clancy's mule, my lady." The general had clearly passed the limits some time ago.

Rose didn't stop to knock. Morning visitors would be arriving very soon. Hurst could carry off just about any calamity with calm, but even his talents would be tested by greeting callers with a storming argument proceeding in the next room.

"What is wrong?" Rose asked as soon as she'd closed the door behind her.

Aunt Paige sat bolt upright in her favorite chair, her hands gripping the ends of the wooden arms like talons. "Nothing but a demonstration of male pride," she declared.

"Pride? You talk of pride?" The general, in civilian clothes, took hasty strides before the fireplace, his hands clasped tightly in the small of his back. "I'm greeted this morning by the news that my fiancée's house has been attacked by a scofflaw who should have been caught and hung weeks ago. I rush to her side to renew my offers of tenderest devotion, and she claims she doesn't need me."

"I never said that," Paige answered. "I said your protection wouldn't have made any difference."

"Of course it would have. That dastard never would have dared step foot in this house if a man lived in it."

"You're being illogical," Paige said, as if she'd said it several times already. "There *are* men living here. Hurst, the footman, the boot boy, and Rupert."

"Rupert? He was on the toddle last night. I saw him at Peck's myself."

"You were at Peck's?"

"I met several of my old officers there for a dinner."

"So you weren't here?"

"How could I be here? I told you . . ."

"Then it wouldn't have made any difference if you were living here or not. The Black Mask—if it was indeed he—chose a time when most of the inhabitants were not at home. Obviously, he'd been watching the house for who knows how long."

"Ah!" The general's face, intent with impending triumph, must have looked very similar on the battlefield. "If I were living here, I'd have soon sent the spalpeen on his way. Aye, and put my boot in his backside for good measure."

Paige slumped as though exhausted. Shaking her head in disbelief, she glanced at Rose. "What was it you said about men being incalculable?"

"I've spent my entire life with men," the general said. "I've marched them and fought with them and taken mess with them three times a day for nearly forty years. I can tell you, my lady, I'd rather fight a battalion of men than have a simple conversation with a woman. They're illogical."

"There is the door, sir. Your precious mankind awaits you."

The general stared at her, his anger fading to dismay. Then pride came to stiffen his backbone. "Very well, my lady. Good morning."

Rose, hating to see the back of the general, touched Paige's hand. When her aunt glanced up, Rose, frowning, shook her head, then nodded toward Sir Augustus. Paige, lips tight, thought for an instant. "Oh, Augustus, don't be silly. I'm sorry."

He paused with his hand on the knob. "It's true, though. You don't need me. You have everything you want."

"Yes, I do."

"Your husbands left you independent."

"Yes, they did."

"I . . . I think I should leave London, Paige. I have a little estate in Cork. I should go to see how it has fared after the winter. An absent landlord's not good for the land or the people. I'm thinking about living there."

Paige's posture had again stiffened, but this time

the rigidity was not of anger. Looking at her aunt's face, Rose saw not a trace of impatience or ire. Instead, she seemed paralyzed by indecision. Even Rose realized this was the moment in which Paige must make up her mind whether to keep to her free widowhood or to throw it away in reckless surrender.

Rose wished she'd not intruded.

Fourteen

They insisted on thanking her, as though their engagement were somehow her doing. Sir Augustus claimed, then and there, the permanent title of uncle. Rose wanted only to escape, to leave them to their happiness. Hurst's announcement of a morning caller gave her an excuse to leave Paige and Augustus alone. Something in their blissful, slightly stunned expressions made her feel very lonely indeed.

Rose managed to give the impression of attending to Ariadne and her mother, who had come to invite her to a house visit in the country. Rose gave an evasive answer and hailed with pleasure the appearance of two of her large admirers. Ariadne clearly wanted to stay, and Rose encouraged her to do so. Her mother did not seem too put out by this. Rose recalled that Ariadne had two younger sisters on the brink of their own bows to society.

When the hour for calls had passed, Rose learned from Hurst that the general had also left the house. The butler was carrying out of the drawing room two used glasses and an unfurled bottle of champagne.

Paige embraced her niece, kissing her on both cheeks. "My word, what have I done? Cork, for heaven's sake. I don't even know what to wear."

"Does it matter? The general won't notice."

"Of course it matters. I'm a bride again, may the
Lord have mercy upon me. I shall need all new nightclothes and underthings, at any rate."

"Why?"

Paige's cheeks turned pink. "Brides and matrons
wear different styles. Oh, you know what I mean. As a
widow, I've been wearing very modest, very boring
nightclothes. No one sees them but me and my maid.
But a husband is a different matter."

"I haven't noticed that your underclothes are particularly boring. They're more interesting than mine,"
she said, thinking of her cashmere dressing gown and
how she'd wished it were floating cambric and delicate lace.

"We shall buy you some new things as well. Madame
Corant has the most charming Moravian white-work
petticoats. Remind me to pick up a few pairs of stockings too. Pink, if she has them."

Before they could go shopping, however, the general returned with a meek man carrying a large black
case under his arm. He bowed to Paige and Rose.
Undoing hasps and clasps, he opened the case to expose row after row of sparkling, gleaming rings. The
sunlight rebounded off them as though the little man
had opened a case full of water, sending rippling rib-
bons of light around the room.

"By Jove," Rupert said, " 'ware Black Mask."

"Oh, we never worry about thieves," the man said,
smilingly nudging the case toward Paige.

"I should say not," Uncle Augustus put in. "There's
a fellow outside who follows this one everywhere he
goes. He's roughly the size of a cart horse." He leaned
over Paige's shoulder. "Pick whichever you like, my
love."

"Augustus, this is unnecessary," she whispered.

"Unnecessary? Certainly not. You must have an engagement ring. Knock their eyes out down at Almack's tonight when I show the prize I've carried off in their teeth."

Flattered, Paige finally chose a yellow diamond set about with brilliants. It slipped onto her slender finger as though it had been made for her. The little man from Rundell and Bridge bowed all around, shook hands with the general, and departed.

Riding in the barouche to her dressmaker's, Paige gazed at her new ring, turning it this way and that in the spring sunshine. "It is beautiful," she said like one determined to tell the truth even if it meant the rack.

"Exquisite," Rose agreed. "And so unusual."

"He's jealous, I'm afraid."

"Jealous? Of whom?"

"Of my other husbands, I think." She pulled on her lavender kid gloves, easing the fingercase over her ring. "He wants to give me more than they ever did. I've tried to tell him he gives me more happiness, but I believe he thought I was being kind."

"Were you?"

She waved at an acquaintance who swept off his hat to bow as she passed. "No, I wasn't. I wonder if he'll ever believe me."

"If you tell him often enough, he will. Why did you accept him, Aunt Paige? I thought you'd made up your mind . . ."

"I think it must be the way he calls me 'my lady' when he is displeased with me. If the only way to make him stop is to marry him, well then, what choice have I?"

Happiness seemed to make people want to spend money. Rose's task on this happy day was to approve Aunt Paige's taste and attempt to keep her from buying too much for her niece. At times, Paige seemed confused as to whose trousseau she was buying, choosing just as many chemises, stockings, and new-style gored petticoats for Rose as she did for herself.

Rose asked to be excused from accompanying Paige and Augustus to Almack's. Though she told herself she didn't wish to play gooseberry, a different motive was at work. The Black Mask had attempted to enter the house quite early yesterday. If he came back again, she didn't want to miss him.

Tonight, the house breathed out silence. The ticking of the clock seemed to have an echo that dragged out the passing seconds into minutes. Rupert went out, promising to be good. Hurst brought her a small tea tray at ten o'clock, and Rose instructed him not to wait up for his mistress. He retreated behind the green baize door with the other servants. The silence grew deeper, as though a fog came creeping in to muffle all sound. Rose read until the heroine's adventures palled beside her own.

Not naturally patient, Rose remembered keeping vigil beside her mother's bed when she'd been so ill. The nights had dragged then as well, but at least there'd been small tasks to do. It was then she had attempted to learn to knit, but it had not been a success. Crochet came more easily. She wished she had her hook and bobbin now.

At least she could light the fire to warm the increasingly chilly air. Hurst had laid it all out on the grate. She had only to light the balls of crumpled paper. Once they caught, she continued to kneel beside the fire, holding her hands out, watching the paper crisp and crumble, seeing how the tips of the kindling began to smolder, smoke, and burn. When they were well alight, she took the poker to push it all under the main logs, smiling as the sparks flew upward.

"Don't you have servants for that?"

His voice teased her. The street accent faded and grew strong by turns. She felt if it would only disappear entirely, she could place it. It sounded so familiar, had sounded familiar even last night.

Turning her head slightly, Rose could just glimpse his dulled boots. "I like to do things for myself." She sent her gaze up to reach his face. "But for some things I need help. Have you decided if you are going to help me?"

He reached down, and Rose put her hand in his to let him pull her to her feet. He held her hand a moment longer, brushing his thumb idly over the sensitive back. "You trust me?" he said softly.

"It is far from sensible, but yes, yes I do."

Behind the mask, his eyes were intent. Rose found her breath catching, her pulse beating more strongly. She recognized the feeling of anticipation as the same she'd known in the instant before he kissed her. "It was you at the Yarborough party."

"I told you it was not." He let go of her hand and turned away, striding across the room. Opening the door to the hall, he glanced out and then gently closed it. "There's not much time. Listen. Tomorrow, precisely at eight o'clock, I want you to be entering Sir Niles's house."

"How am I to do that? Through the window?"

"No. Through the door. Knock or ring. His man will let you in."

"Oh, of course. I'm sorry. I thought you meant something more spectacular."

"Would you truly climb in through a window?"

"You do."

"That's a different case all together. I'm a thief. It's what I do. Miss."

Rose smiled sunnily at him, which seemed to make him nervous. "Some people say you are a Robin Hood."

"Some people will say anything."

"You did give that emerald tiara to that poor man."

"It was paste. Why d'you think he couldn't fence it?"

"Fence . . . oh, sell it?"

"That's right. You pick up the cant right quick."

"It's not that difficult. You see, perhaps my talents lie along yours." Even Rose couldn't tell how serious she was being. "You could teach me to be a thief, couldn't you?"

"I'm not lookin' to take on no apprentices," he said. He roughened his voice, seemingly as an afterthought.

Rose wanted him to go on talking. "So tell me what it is I must do."

"You go 'round to Sir Niles's house just on eight. While he's busy with you, I'll nip into his room and take ahold of his strongbox."

"You sound certain it's in his bedroom."

"Certain sure. You just keep him occupied."

"What about the servants?"

"What about yours? They don't have any idea you aren't alone. I come and go at will in any house I choose."

"How did you learn to do that? Were you apprenticed to another thief?"

"I . . ." Suddenly a finger flew to his lips in a universal sign for silence. Footsteps crossed the hall. As a good servant, Hurst did not knock. No sooner had the knob begun to turn than Black Mask, swiftly and above all silently, slipped across the floor to whisk himself out of sight behind the opening, sheltering door.

"I beg your pardon, Miss Spenser."

"Yes, what is it?" Rose asked, trying to pretend she often stood idly in the middle of a room late at night.

"I disremember—you understand how it is when one is readying to retire for the night—I cannot quite call to my memory whether Sir Augustus is partial to burgundy."

"I haven't the slightest idea. Is it important?"

"I am attempting to choose the wines for tomorrow evening's dinner."

"Dinner?" Rose asked, willing herself not to cast even a suspicion of a glance at the door. "What time are you serving?"

"I thought eight o'clock, miss, since her ladyship prefers not to keep country hours."

"Don't lay a place for me, Hurst. I think I have an engagement for eight o'clock."

"With Miss Ariadne Belmont? A very pleasant spoken young lady, if I may say so. An excellent family." The butler frowned as he spoke and Rose stiffened.

"What is it, Hurst?"

"You should have rung if you wished the fire lit, Miss." He crossed to the fireplace, went down on his knees with a chuff of effort, and began to jab at the logs with the poker. "You've got to let the air in," he said.

Rose watched, torn between alarm and laughter, as the Black Mask slipped around the door and through the opening. He did it so quickly, Rose could hardly believe she'd seen him go. After one instant, he reappeared only long enough to kiss his hand to her and hold up eight fingers. She nodded eagerly.

The next morning, Colonel Wapton appeared among the morning visitors for the first time in days. His former meticulous appearance had been restored, and yet something hunted in his eyes told Rose all was not yet well with the officer. He'd hardly taken time to make polite inquiries of her health before drawing her aside. "Is it safe? The . . . my satchel, is it safe?"

"Yes, I have it inside . . ."

"Don't say it," he said on a frantic note. He smiled uneasily at the other men in the room, some of whom stared when his voice had risen. Even the general, keeping vigil over his fiancée, frowned at him despite his pinkish haze of happiness.

"I don't want anyone to know where you've hidden it," he said, his gaze flicking, animal-like, to the faces around him. "I'll come for it tonight."

"Tonight I shall not be at home," Rose said haughtily. The colonel hadn't even asked if it would be convenient to pick up his satchel tonight. He'd given the order as if she were a non-too-bright subaltern. "I will happily leave instructions that you are to be given your property upon application to our butler. Now, pray excuse me, Colonel. I believe my aunt requires me."

All day, Rose would, at unexpected moments, feel a pulse of excitement quickening through her veins. Her intentions were of the best, but it was not good intentions that made her feel as though she'd swallowed a hot-air balloon. She felt as though she should keep a tight grasp on the furniture lest she float up into the air.

She played over and over with the details of how she'd make her way to Sir Niles's home, what she would say, and how he would talk to her. Though not

an easy man to know, she had the memory of their
tête-à-têtes to buoy her up. At some point, she'd discovered she could talk easily and naturally to him
when he forgot his consequence. If her luck held, tomorrow night might prove to be one of those times.

"You seem all lit up," Paige said during their noon
meal. "I thought only brides-to-be wore such a glow. Is
there something you are not telling me?"

Rose left her seat to kiss her aunt. "I'm so happy for
you, though a little sad for me. So much for my dream
of living in London with you."

"I am sorry for that . . ." Paige began.

"I'm only teasing. How could I repine when I see
how happy you are? No one deserves happiness more
than you, dearest of aunts."

As the hours passed, creeping slowly toward eight,
Rose became more restless. More difficulties seemed
to throng her imagination with each passing tick of
the clock. What could she say to Sir Niles? First, of
course, she must pass the point of explaining why precisely she'd come in so unorthodox a manner.
Perhaps she could raise the issue of Rupert's debt
again. Rose no sooner thought that than she recoiled.
She wished the matter could be forgotten between
them. But once she had them in her hands, having so
deceived Sir Niles to gain them, there could never be
friendship between them anymore. The thought had
not occurred to her before, since she was generally
honest, and suddenly she felt unaccountably close to
tears. She would gain Rupert a breathing spell, but
she would lose Niles.

As though she were choosing what she'd wear to
the guillotine, she deliberated a long time, knowing
misty pink silk and her best silver-shot shawl were undoubtedly too dressy for a clandestine call upon a

single gentleman. Yet she discarded everything else as being far too ordinary for such a desperate adventure.

Despite her depression over the deception she had to perform, Rose slipped out of the house at a quarter to eight. Aunt Paige had gone with Sir Augustus to a small dinner party while Rupert, still recuperating from the night before, stayed in his room. Rose rapped on his door to reiterate her story about Mrs. Belmont taking her along to an evening with Ariadne, but he didn't seem to care.

As soon as the front door closed behind her, Rose felt the night close around her. Her footsteps sounded particularly loud while the slight breeze, carrying the scent of rain, caught at her shawl, tugging at it like an impatient child. If being alone in a garden at night had been mildly thrilling, being alone on the street at night made her feel strangely exposed and threatened. She glanced over her shoulder, afraid she heard someone following.

Pulling up in front of her aunt's door was a traveling chaise with a pair of horses. A militarily-shouldered man in street clothes had just emerged and was climbing the stairs. Rose recognized Colonel Wapton come to call for his precious satchel.

With a petulant sniff, Rose walked on, hurrying now for fear he'd turn his head and see her. She felt a strange sense of relief as she turned the corner out of his line of sight.

Before she reached the next corner, the mist in the air had thickened, clinging to her hair and clothing, collecting to drip down her cheek.

When she reached Sir Niles's door, it had begun to rain. "So much for this dress," Rose said, and all but ran up the front steps. A slight overhang gave her a measure of shelter.

The chimes and bells of London were calling the hour, the deep tolling and sharp tings alike muffled by the mist.

After smoothing her hair and giving her shawl a controlling tug, Rose rapped smartly upon the front door. She prepared a brilliant smile, ready to charm whoever opened the door into letting her enter unquestioned.

When the moments passed and no one came, her smile slowly grew rigid and faded out. Standing forlornly on the doorstep, cold and wet, was not part of her imagined entrance.

Mustering her courage once again, she knocked as forcefully as her gloves would permit. She heard a scrabbling, hasty series of sounds from within.

"Hello?" she called.

Again silence. Just when she felt ready to turn tail, the scraping metallic sound of the moving lock reached her. The large knob in the center of the door began to turn, slowly, slowly. This was more terrifying than the noises. She didn't know who or what would answer.

When the pale, bony face of Sir Niles's man poked forward through a tiny opening, Rose almost laughed. "Is Sir Niles at home?"

"Y-yes."

"Then kindly stand aside and let me in."

Unbelievably, the valet still hesitated. "I—um—do you have an appointment?"

Rose drew herself up, suppressing the shivers that had begun to travel over her. "Kindly stand aside." She started forward and the thin man, looking like a wasp in his damp yellow and black striped apron, fell back before her.

"Please tell Sir Niles that Miss Spenser has called."

"Oh, I . . ."

Behind him, double doors suddenly opened inward. Sir Niles stood between them, looking much as he had on the night he helped her over the wall. His hair, however, was disarranged and looked wet, as if he had held his head under a pump and then pushed the waves of deep brown back with his hands.

"Pray enter, Miss Spenser. Baxter doesn't mean to be inhospitable. Brandy, Baxter. And a towel for Miss Spenser."

"Yes, sir."

"Won't you join me?" Niles asked, gesturing toward the room behind him. The dark paneling of the library seemed to absorb all the light afforded by several branches of candles. Rose gravitated toward the fire leaping in a wide fireplace, the marble mantel supported by two fauns, black and deep red by turns as the firelight caught a uplifted horn or shaggy thigh.

Remembering that the Black Mask had asked her to keep Sir Niles occupied, Rose's imagination quailed now that she stood in the same room with him. What could she do that would keep him from going to his bedroom? Throwing herself into his arms, an image that came to her with shocking vividness, would be out of the question.

"I'm sorry to disturb you so late."

"Always a pleasure."

"Oh, don't," she said suddenly, knowing this was the last time they'd ever meet without constraint on her side. "Don't we know each other well enough by this time to dispense with all this empty formality? Can't we be friends?"

The flickering light made his eyes seem deep set and dark. "Friends? Why should we . . ."

A thunderous knocking interrupted him. Before anyone could go to answer, the front door burst open and two men, struggling, striving each to hold the other back, stormed in.

"Let me go, Spenser," Colonel Wapton demanded. "I tell you, he's here! I saw him . . ."

"You can't come bursting into a man's house like this. A man's home is a castle and all that."

"To hell with that." The colonel shook off Rupert like a bull mastiff tiring of the gambols of a puppy. He headed toward the rear of Sir Niles's house.

"Sir Niles!" Rupert stood in the middle of the hall and called. "I say, Wapton, you can't go upstairs in another man's house like that." He seemed to throw himself forward, and there came the noise of a renewed struggle. A crash indicated that a reception table had fallen over.

Rose, the instant she recognized her brother, shrank back against the far side of the fireplace, instinctively choosing to conceal herself. Suddenly the consideration she'd dismissed—the unconventionality of visiting a single gentleman—appeared to her through Rupert's eyes. He might even attempt to call Sir Niles out. Or, just as great an evil, Sir Niles might feel compelled to offer for her. Though she could trust Sir Niles not to accept Rupert's challenge, she didn't know if she could trust herself to turn down what she now knew she wanted above all things. If only she could stop the Black Mask, she thought, but knew it must already be too late.

"If you reach along to your right," Niles said quickly and softly, "the second bookcase along is actually a door."

She nodded as Rupert called out Niles's name again, this time thickly, as though his mouth were half covered. "I'd better go," Niles said, watching her as she found the moving shelf. "There are some rather nice objects out in the hall."

Another shattering crash didn't even make him wince. "A Chinese vase." A more ringing noise came a second later, accompanied by a cry of pain. "And a silver bowl."

"Go, before they ruin your house!" Rose said, wondering why he didn't seem to care about his precious things. Why would a man stand smiling at her as if he'd been handed a much-desired gift when two ruffians were holding a mill in his foyer? A slight spark of hope lit in her heart.

He spun on his heel abruptly. The next thing she heard was Rupert greeting him with relief and a touch of chagrin. "Thank God you're home, Niles. Help me with this madman, will you?"

"Let him up, Rupert."

Rose could not resist stealing a glance at this scene. She peered out of the library. Fortunately, Niles and Rupert had their backs to her, and Wapton was holding his hand to his eye. "You've got to let me search," he said desperately. "I know he's here. I saw him!"

"Who is?" Niles asked.

Rupert broke in. "I was walking in the door at my aunt's home when he all but knocks me down in the street. He claims he saw the Black Mask in my sister's bedroom. Of all the crust! What the hell was Wapton doing in my sister's bedroom?"

"I told you." Wapton took his hand down to look at his fingertips, then gingerly felt his brow. "The butler called me to come up."

"I didn't see Hurst anywhere," Rupert said suspiciously.

"I sent him downstairs again when we found . . .

what I was looking for. Then I turned to go and there was the Black Mask standing in front of me. As soon as he saw me, he bolted."

"I fail to see," Niles said at his most drawling, "what this has to do with your intrusion."

"Why, he climbed over the wall at the back of this house. He could be hiding anywhere."

"He's probably halfway to the Seven Dials by now," Rupert pointed out, scoffing. "Why would he hide here, of all places? A criminal like that would head back to his lair at once like any wild beast."

"Undoubtedly true," Niles said, "though my recollection of natural history is not the strongest. I haven't the least objection to your searching my house, Wapton. I shall call my man to help you, but first let me offer you some brandy. You are undoubtedly overset."

"No. Thank you," Wapton said, half turning in his seat to cast a glance up the staircase. "I'll start at once."

"Come, come," Niles said. "If the fellow's here, he's not going anywhere. Come into the library."

Shaking her head a little at the incalculability of men, even those she loved, Rose slipped through the concealed doorway to find herself in a kind of butler's pantry. The brandy Niles had sent his man for sat on the counter, bottle gleaming, glasses bright. Of Baxter, however, there was no sign.

Rose started forward, looking for the man to help her out of the back premises. She would circle around to the front and reenter, feigning surprise and shock at finding Rupert and the colonel there before her. She could also tell Baxter to put another glass on his silver tray.

She found Baxter by the constant, low muttering of "oh, dear, oh, dear." He hardly seemed to know what he was doing. As she came around a corner, she saw him, a bundle of wet clothing clasped to his chest which explained the damp spot on his apron. A piece jerked from the top of this pile and unfolded as it fell, revealing it to be a black stock. With a shake of his head, he bent to pick it up. His movements were encumbered by a rain-darkened leather satchel under his arm.

As he placed the fallen stock on the top of the pile, another piece dropped from underneath. "Oh, dear. What next?"

"Let me help you, Baxter," Rose said.

When he jumped in surprise, his hands flew up. Everything in his arms tumbled. Rose, feeling as if the earth had stopped turning and begun to spin the other way, reached down for one very familiar thing.

Fifteen

"You are welcome to search," Niles said, "providing, of course, that Rupert accompanies you."

Both men's coats and heads were darkened with rain. Wapton passed his hand over his face, wiping away both the rain and his panic. A low, boiling anger took its place. "Perhaps you can explain, Sir Niles, where the Black Mask has disappeared to."

"Tell me what you saw in greater detail."

"A man, all in black, masked. About your height or a tad taller. He . . . ran as soon as he saw me. I gave chase, naturally."

"I saw no one," Rupert repeated. "Just this fellow charging down the stairs like Hannibal's elephant. We collided, and I'm glad now I got some of my own back. He put his dashed elbow in my eye." He tapped his cheekbone experimentally. "Shouldn't be surprised if I have a blasted black eye."

"The Black Mask ran through Lady Marlton's house, showing great familiarity with the premises," Wapton said.

"What's that? Listen, if you dare cast any aspersions on my aunt . . ."

"I didn't mean that. This is a clever thief; he might have studied the house before he ever entered it.

Meanwhile, while we stand here debating, he's getting away."

"On your own showing," Niles put in silkily, "he hasn't stolen anything, so why go through the exhaustion of chasing him?" He watched Wapton closely, though his eyes were purposefully sleepy.

The man chewed his lip as he internally debated confession. "He did steal something. Something of mine."

"He did?" Instantly, Rupert was contrite. "I'm sorry to hear that, old man. That explains why you were off like a hound on the scent. What was it?"

"Yes," Niles said. "What was it?"

Wapton seemed to have some constriction in his throat. "Merely a bundle of old papers. I daresay the fellow will toss them on the nearest fire once he realizes they have no value." It was not hot in the hall, but sweat inched glisteningly down Wapton's cheek.

"Not incriminating, I hope," Rupert said with a loud laugh. "Else they'll be on the prime minister's desk come the morning."

Niles saw Wapton grow pale, though he tried to join in with Rupert's laugh. The man's smile could have been the rictus of a man ten days dead. Feeling just one pang of pity, Niles renewed his offer of brandy. This time, both men accepted.

The tray, with a bottle and three glasses, sat on the wide library table. He saw no sign of Baxter. Surely, his man would escort Rose safely to her aunt's house as soon as he himself had herded Wapton and Rupert out of the hall.

Niles felt he had lost control of this situation at roughly the time Rose had walked in. He'd expected her, having instructed her to arrive at just that time, yet her entrance had been some kind of trigger for chaos. He felt like a juggler, competent at passing four clubs from hand to hand, suddenly asked to add three flaming torches, two anvils, and a clutch of hummingbird eggs.

Wapton, after knocking back his brandy with a cavalier disregard for its age and quality, began to stride about the room. Niles leaned against the desk and watched him, his arms crossed. Every so often, he noticed, Wapton shot him a wondering glance, gradually sharpening into suspicion. Niles thought about how to play the scene he felt fast approaching.

Rupert reached for the ring-necked decanter as soon as he'd drunk his first glass. "Still want to know what the hell Hurst meant by letting you go up to m'sister's room. He's a stickler for the conventions, I know." He drank. "And then to leave you alone up there. That ain't like him."

"I can't say I've studied the inner workings of a butler's mind as you seem to have done, Spenser. Are you setting up as an expert?" Wapton sneered impatiently.

"You've got a damned insulting tone," Rupert said, rising.

"Sit down, Rupert," Niles said out of the corner of his mouth. "You seem to have something you wish to say to me, Wapton."

The colonel squinted at Niles. "Why is your hair wet?"

Rupert stared. "You know why. The skies opened as we came up the street. I'm not prepared to swear it wasn't hailing."

"Not yours, fool. His. You're the right height, Alardyce. You could have climbed that wall and been safe in your house in seconds."

Again, Rupert spoke first. "Sir Niles the Black Mask? You're all about in your head, Wapton. He couldn't be."

"Why not?" Wapton said. "He's famous for his gem collection, which the Black Mask hasn't even attempted to steal. No one would suspect the meticulous Sir Niles Alardyce of climbing in windows and over dirty rooftops."

"I certainly wouldn't," Rupert agreed, reaching for the brandy decanter once more.

Wapton approached Niles, his shoulders squared, looking like a whole battalion on the march. He would have made two of Niles. His clenched fists looked like hammers. "Give it back, Alardyce, and I won't waste time beating you to a bloody pulp."

"Yes, you haven't much time to waste, do you, Wapton?" Though his body had tensed, Niles kept his voice level and easy. "You've surely a long way to travel. Which way are you going? The Continent? Or the Americas? What kennel have you chosen to hide in, your tail between your legs?"

He couldn't filter out of his tone the contempt he felt, and Wapton's lips twisted into a grimace compounded of anger and anticipation.

Slowly, Niles straightened up and readied himself, fire and exhilaration flickering in his veins. At last, he could take physical revenge for everything Christian had suffered. Wapton was big, but Niles had learned from his earliest boyhood that agility and speed could defeat strength and size.

"I could forgive you for stealing my papers," Wapton said in a growl, "if you hadn't dragged Rose into your schemes. I'm going to enjoy this."

Rupert blinked in surprise. "What's that? What the devil are you saying about my sister?"

"How did Alardyce know to steal my papers from her room? He must have been there."

"Here now . . ."

"Maybe if you weren't drunk three nights out of four, Spenser, you'd know what goes on in that house. For all you know, Alardyce seduced her weeks ago. I would have kept her safe from the likes of him."

Niles hit him. The big man staggered back, the back of his hand flying to the trickle of blood that came from his split lip. Niles ignored the pain of his knuckles. "Don't try to make yourself out the hero of this melodrama," he said. "You're the villain. You've been the villain all along, you and Beringer and Curtman."

"Here," Rupert said, trying to keep up. "I know those names. Poets, aren't they?"

"I don't know what you mean," Wapton said so weakly that even Rupert looked contemptuous. He turned his back on him.

"Listen, Sir Niles, I know you've never so much as looked at my sister . . ."

"You're quite wrong."

"What? Now, see here, if you've been playing fast and loose with Rose, you'll have to take the consequences."

"I'm entirely prepared to do so, Rupert, but there are a few other matters I must deal with first."

"I beg your pardon," Rose said in a voice so clear and icy that it instantly chilled the virility-fueled confrontation in the library. Wapton and Rupert looked in her direction, pausing as if frozen in their positions. The only sound was Rupert's glass hitting the floor, dropped from nerveless fingers.

Niles turned his head much more slowly, his eyes closed, delaying the inevitable moment when he'd witness the wreck of his hopes. When he did finally look at Rose, she was no wrathful maiden, but stood there in the shadows smiling at him with such warmth and tenderness as to make his rage dissolve like a pinch of salt in the sea.

She crossed the room to his side, taking his bruised hand tenderly in hers, bringing it to rest against her bosom. "You are quite wrong, Colonel. Niles isn't the Black Mask. He couldn't be. He's been right here with me the entire evening. As for his hair being a trifle damp, I have cause to know he took a bath a little while ago."

Niles, appalled, tried to tug his hand free, though an instant ago he'd been more than pleased with its location.

"How do you know that?" Wapton demanded.

She lowered her eyelids demurely. Was it a trick of the firelight or was she actually blushing? "Really, Colonel . . ." she said softly.

"Rose!" Rupert cried.

"I'm sorry, Rupert. I know how this must look."

"It looks as though you've lost your mind," her brother said in anguish. "Wapton's right. This is all my fault. Sir Niles, you must marry her at once."

Niles started to speak but Rose gripped his hand so tightly, her nails left marks. "No," Rose said in all seriousness. "I make my own decisions."

Rupert looked as if he didn't know whether to hit Niles or break down and cry. "What will Father say? And poor Aunt Paige? How could you betray her trust like this?"

"Why don't you go tell her?" Rose suggested.

"I will. I'll tell her I have a sister who is entirely dead to shame!" He marched toward the library doors, only to wheel sharply before he reached them. Rose, who had sighed with relief at his departure, tensed again. "Where is she dining tonight?"

"With the Gardners."

"Middle of St. James Square?" At her nod, he marched off again.

Niles felt Rose's body sag against his as she watched her brother leave the room. She let go of his hand but he turned it in his own and brought it to his lips. "He was in no danger, Rose," he murmured. "Wapton wants to kill me, not Rupert."

"He'll never do it," she answered back, brightly. "But I want to see you mill him down."

Wapton sneered. "That runt? I was division boxing champion three years running."

"I've already hit you once," Niles said, untying his sash.

"That was luck."

"I've always had lucky hands," Niles said, handing his dressing gown to Rose, along with the scarf he wore about his neck. Under it, he had on scuffed boots and black breeches.

Though it was piling scandal on scandal, Rose watched him dance out, his fists ready. His body, though slender, had muscles that gleamed like oiled stones under his smooth skin. As he turned his shoulder to Wapton, presenting less of a target, she saw a line of dark hair ran down the center of his chest into the waist of his breeches over a ridged belly. His body had the condition of a marble Greek god.

Wapton huffed as he struggled out of his damp coat. "We'll see if she'll still want you when your pretty face is battered and your nose is spread over half your face." He ripped off his military-style stock and yanked his shirt out of his waistband. He started to take it off but glanced at Rose, who was gazing with admiration at Niles's lean form. He left his shirt on, but sucked in his stomach.

He danced out as well, shaking his arms and shoulders to loosen them. "I'm going to destroy you," he said levelly.

"Enough talking." Niles's eyes gleamed with satisfaction and a kind of unholy joy. Rose's faith in him didn't waver but she did close her eyes as Wapton swung his left.

She'd sometimes gone to the butcher's at home. The sound she heard reminded her of when the butcher cut off a chop with one heavy stroke of the cleaver.

She opened her eyes to see Wapton staggering back, doubled over. Niles followed him, his boots tapping rapidly over the floor. Then he slipped in a small puddle of brandy from Rupert's dropped glass. The crystal rolled ringingly across the floor.

Hope blazing in his eyes, Wapton came forward, his hands held low, his teeth showing. Rose suddenly knew what a man who meant to kill looked like. She wanted to scream, but pressed her fist hard against her lips, stifling any distracting sound.

Niles twisted like a fish leaping out of the water and saved himself from falling. Shadows moved across their bodies as they weaved in and out of candlelight and firelight, teasing eyes and intellect. Wapton threw out his right but somehow Niles was no longer in the same place to be hit.

Three blows later—two to the belly, one to the jaw—Wapton went over like a felled oak. His eyelids fluttered and his feet and arms still moved restlessly, but for the rest, he had lost all consciousness.

Niles shook his right hand as if moving it very fast would keep the pain from finding him. Judging by his grimace, he didn't succeed.

Rose flew across the room to him. "Niles. Are you hurt?"

"It feels good," he said, smiling at her. "It feels right."

The warmth and tenderness he showed brought unaccountable tears into her eyes. "I was so afraid."

"You? I've never seen you show fear."

"You weren't looking at me. And it's a good thing, as it turns out."

Niles laid his bruised right hand along her cheek. Rose nestled her face against his palm, her eyes closing in delight. "What are you going to do with the colonel?" she asked.

"What colonel?" Niles tilted her face up, eager to claim openly what he'd only stolen before. Yet no sooner had he dipped his head down to taste her lips than Rose gently moved his hand away and stepped back. "Rose?" Niles said, disappointed.

"I have something to show you first," she said. "What did I . . ." She hurried over to the "secret" panel, really no more than an easy access way to the butler's pantry. She snatched up something dark from the floor. Turning her back, she put her hand to her face. When she spun around, her eyes were shaded by the mask that covered her from cheek to brow.

"I'm afraid your man gave the show away," she said. "You see, I know the colonel was right about you. You are the Black Mask."

"Yes. I am." He moved around the table to reach for his shirt.

"Why this game, Niles? I think I have a right to know, and not only because you decoyed me out of my room tonight so you could steal the colonel's papers." She laughed a little. "And I thought I was being so clever, enticing you to come to me by using the Malikzadi."

"Oh, that reminds me." He reached into his dress-

ing gown's pocket and put the world's ugliest ruby
ring into the center of his desk. It clashed horribly
with the greenish color of his desk blotter.

"You did steal it? Why?"

"So you would think I only took the satchel as an afterthought." He took up the ring, held it in his hand
a moment, then placed it again on the desk.

Rose came a little closer. "That's not my ring."

"No. I had that one made a few weeks ago. It's not
fit for a queen, but perhaps a bride?" Rose could
never have imagined that the arrogant Sir Niles, who
had just decommissioned a man twice his size, could
look so humble and nervous.

She reached out and took up the ring. Like the Malikzadi, the center stone was a ruby. This one,
however, flashed with a passionate red flame, surrounded by brilliants. She slipped it onto the third
finger of her left hand. "It fits."

Taking off the mask, she put it in the spot the ring
had been. "I don't know yet if I can do what you ask
me, Niles. I have guessed some of what you were
doing, but not everything. Tell me everything."

"It seems my mask was wearing thin."

"A trifle." Searching his expression for a clue to his
feelings was unprofitable. "I don't understand why . . ."

"Why the meticulous Sir Niles Alardyce would do so
quixotic a thing as become a thief by night?" He sat
down on a deeply buttoned leather sofa a few feet away
from where Colonel Wapton slumbered with noisy
breaths. Rose came over to sit beside him. Though it
was forward of her, she took his hand and held it com-
fortingly between her own, the ruby ring on top.

"You remember my telling you about Christian?"

"Your cousin."

"Yes. How we both entered the army?"

"That's right. He died?"

"Yes, but not honorably on the field. He died in prison, clapped up for the crime of selling guns to the enemy."

"He was innocent!"

Niles smiled at her, but there was pain behind his eyes. He sighed. "No. He wasn't. He definitely had a hand in the crime. But even the authorities couldn't swallow the idea that Christian had planned and executed the series of misdirection, inventory swapping, and painstaking deliveries that took place, despite the fact someone had very carefully falsified documents to show he was the principal criminal."

"Wapton, Beringer, and Curtman?" Rose looked with loathing at the snoring man at her feet.

"Exactly. Christian's commanding officer believed it, too, but there was no evidence. That's why Christian wasn't hanged outright but put in prison."

"How did he die?"

"Typhoid broke out. Bad air and appalling conditions will let that happen. Christian worked as a nurse in the prison, caught it himself, and died. They buried him with the other prisoners instead of letting me bring him home." He stared into the fire as if seeing evil visions in the flames.

"I swore I'd ferret out the other three and expose them. I didn't realize what else they'd been doing in the years since then. Wapton changed regiments but stayed in the service, rising in rank year by year. Beringer and Curtman left the service with several thousand pounds waiting for them in England, but they couldn't rest like honest men. Mr. Crenshaw helped me track them down through the ports, the banks, and his own band of cronies down at the Inns of Court."

Thinking of the ruminative attorney, Rose could

smile despite her tears. "I suppose your part was to search various houses of ill-repute, thus gaining a renewed reputation as a rake. Did you find out very much about these men that way?"

"If I say 'yes,' will you believe me?"

Rose couldn't withstand such a searching glance and looked away.

"You know," he said, the tension slipping from him, "you have a charming little dimple in your left cheek that I see only when you are trying not to smile. I always want to kiss you then."

Rose hid that information in her heart to examine later. "But why all this mummery of the Black Mask? Why couldn't you just expose them for what they had already done?"

"There was still no evidence I could take to a judge. I had to find it. But how could I search their houses or offices?" He laughed a little, reminiscently. "I remember how horrified Crenshaw was when I first put forward the suggestion that I turn thief. He was so certain I'd be shot or run through by some enterprising householder."

"What confused me most was that you are so good at housebreaking. That trick with the window at my aunt's home, how did you think of that? There are no books, surely, that tell you how to rob people."

"No books needed when you have a Baxter."

"A Baxter? Your man?"

"A reformed thief, if you please. Known until an unfortunate choice of victim as Beau Blade for his fancy waistcoats, charm of speech, and swordplay. I almost wish Wapton there had gone for a sword. It was a shame to waste Baxter's training."

"Who was his last victim?" Rose asked though she felt she already knew.

"I found him rifling my box of pretties early one afternoon when I returned unexpectedly. Finding his talents to be precisely what I required, I dismissed my former man and learned all I could from Baxter while teaching him the finer points of valeting. I promised him once the three were dealt with, I'd write him a sterling recommendation for his next employer. He's fallen in love with respectability, poor man."

"And you, I suppose, have fallen in love with reckless danger."

"No, my dear. With you." His arm slipped down from the back of the sofa to pull her tightly against him. "I've been going slowly mad for weeks, torn between what I had to finish and what I so longed to begin. Tell me the truth, Rose. I've mistreated you, I know. Can you forgive me?"

"Mistreated? When have you ever mistreated me?"

"At Mrs. Yarborough's party."

"I knew that was you! It's nice to know I'm not a complete fool."

"Is that all you have to say to me?" He settled her a little more closely against his body. Tilting up her face, he kissed her with restraint. When she sighed against his mouth and let go of his hand to touch his neck, he tore away and laid his cheek against hers. "You are the fulfillment of every wish, Rose. I never dreamed I'd find such a wonder."

"Let's finish what we owe to Christian," Rose said, as Wapton groaned and stirred, "before we think about ourselves."

Wapton rolled over onto his side and pushed up onto his elbow. He ran his fingers into his hairline, blinking as if his eyes didn't want to focus correctly. "Christian? Who's talking about that fool?"

"Fool, was he?" Niles was on his feet, standing over his enemy.

"Yes." His tongue moved around his mouth, causing strange bulges and rolling movements. His voice sounded thick. "My teeth feel loose. What did you hit me with, a brick?"

"No, just my fist. I'm willing to do it again, too."

Tasting the blood on his lip, Wapton dabbed at it with the side of his fist. "I know your kind, Alardyce; you won't hit me again. I'm beaten and I know it." He rolled a little more, propping himself up on both elbows, his long legs stretched out before him. He moved his jaw around experimentally. "No one's ever put me down before," he said mildly, his voice recovering. "I'd like to know how you did it."

"I'm damned if I know," Niles said. "I simply wanted to more than I wanted anything else, I suppose."

Wapton nodded. "Pure heart, clean living. Just like they tell you at school. I suppose you want to know about Christian."

"I have the papers, Wapton. You don't need to tell me anything."

"You know he was guilty? Just as guilty as we were, maybe more so because we weren't fools. He trusted us, especially Beringer. We were his friends, his comrades in that dirty business. He really believed in honor among thieves."

"And it killed him."

"He should have known better than to nurse the scum of the prison yard. It's better to be alive than dead, no matter what the circumstances."

Rose shook her head at this true cynicism. "What are you going to do with him?" she asked.

"Going to call in the Runners, Alardyce? I'll spill all your nasty family secrets if you do. What will her parents say to the news that you've got a gaolbird in the family tree?"

"They won't care," Rose said defiantly, though she knew her father would hate it and her mother would never forget it for an instant.

Niles picked up Wapton's coat and threw it into the man's lap. "You're leaving the country, I take it."

"I have a chaise waiting. I was only stopping to pick up my satchel from Miss Spenser and to ask her . . . well, never mind."

"I never would have gone with you," Rose said. "I don't like you."

Niles had to help Wapton to his feet. The man put his hand to his ribs and groaned if he turned or twisted even the slightest amount. "Damn you, I think you've broken one of my ribs."

"Get out," Niles said. "Go to the Continent or the devil. I'll give you thirty-six hours to leave the country and that only because you were somewhat concerned for Rose when you confronted me earlier. If it were not for that, I would turn you over to the Runners or your own commanding officer no matter what threats you made."

Wapton sneered, his open good looks destroyed now that the essential littleness of his soul stood revealed. "You'll never dare give those papers to anyone. They condemn Christian just as much as they do the rest of us."

"With this difference," Niles said. "He's dead and has nothing left to lose."

Rose linked her arm with Niles's as Wapton cast a glance around. "You'd better hurry," she said. "Your thirty-six hours started two minutes ago."

Niles softly closed and locked the door behind him.

"So good riddance to all bad rubbish," he said. "And now, Miss Spenser . . ."

"And now, Sir Niles?"

"Now we begin."

Epilogue

The roads in Ireland were no worse than the roads in England, just appalling in a different way. Mud instead of dust, sheep in the road instead of cows, and long distances between habitations at least enriched the adventure. Rose, however, didn't mind the dirt, the ruts, or the enforced slowness of the drive. She had her baby girl in the coach with her.

She and Niles could spend long hours jouncing Melinda Jane on their knees, gazing into her cornflower blue eyes, or just holding her close as she slept. At home the ruler of the nursery had decreed Melinda should live in the nursery where mothers and fathers were a treat, not an all-day event.

"We'll arrive there today," Niles said, early on the last morning, putting his foot on the coach step and looking at the sky. "Barring accidents like the wheel falling off again."

"Couldn't we miss the turning and continue right on around the whole perimeter of the country?" Rose asked, only half teasing.

"I'm in favor of it, but I think Paige and Augustus would be disappointed. They haven't seen Melinda yet."

"You're right, but these days have been so sweet. I hate to see them end." Rose watched out the coach window as the nursemaid appeared, carrying Melinda bundled in her arms. The majestic nurse, Mrs. Jarricks, walked alone and in state. Even while staying in the sometimes primitive inns, her vast bonnet of tucked and frilled white lawn was thoroughly starched, ironed, and as upstanding as a windmill.

"I'll take the baby, Nancy," Rose called. Mrs. Jarricks's mouth tightened like the drawstring on a reticule.

"I can h'only say h'again that it h'would be better, my lady, to h'allow Miss Melinda to travel with those trained to look h'after her." Mrs. Jarricks never dropped an "h," but she was a great collector of them.

Niles intercepted the nursemaid. "Give her to me."

Little Melinda might be only six months old, but she definitely knew when her father held out his arms to her, she wanted to go. She kicked and gurgled in delight, her toothless smile enchanting.

"Sir Niles, I can h'only remind you that a constant routine is h'essential for h'any child."

"So you've said repeatedly, Mrs. Jarricks, and I quite agree with you. So far on this journey, Melinda has ridden every day with us. That, therefore, is her routine."

Mrs. Jarricks sniffed. If anything, her mouth pursed even more tightly. "H'Ireland is not my choice for a holiday," she said awfully as she strode across the cracked surface of the yard in the direction of the second traveling coach, this one piled high with luggage. "Come, Nancy."

The maid dipped a hasty curtsy and raced after Mrs. Jarricks. Lucy and Baxter, who had retracted his notice as soon as he met Lucy, were already inside and waiting.

Niles handed the baby to Rose, then climb himself. "Drive on, Burrows."

The coachman touched his hat brim with the handle of his whip and ordered the ostler to "stand away from their heads." A few minutes later, the second coach followed, leaving the landlord mourning the early departure of such open-fisted guests.

"You're planning to dismiss her when we go home," Niles said, holding out his finger to Melinda. He was always delighted that she'd hold on so tightly with her little baby fist.

"I won't have to," Rose said. "I feel certain she'll give her notice the moment we sight the dome of St. Paul's."

"I still don't see how you came to hire such a despot."

"You interviewed her, too," Rose reminded him. "You said you wanted firmness."

"Well, she's firm, all right, but she should draw the line at making me feel like a probationary first-year at a particularly Gothic public school."

Rose laughed. "I doubt we are what she had in mind when she applied for a position in gentleman's household."

"We are a ragtag group, and I wouldn't have it any other way." He slid his arm around his wife's back. "Do you mind not having a more regular household?"

Rose gazed at Melinda, her eyes distant. For a moment, she didn't answer.

"Rose, do you mind?"

She pulled out of her abstraction at the urgent note in his voice, and smiled at him. "How can you ask? What would I do with servants equal to my consequence? I can scarcely move about the house as it is."

"What were you thinking of just then?"

Rose cuddled Melinda a little, though the baby was re interested in reaching out toward the large but-

tons on Rose's traveling costume. "I was thinking perhaps I shall ask Nancy to stay on as nurse once Mrs.
Jarricks is gone. She might not have the experience,
but I feel as though she truly loves Melinda which is
more than I can say for Mrs. Jarricks."

"It's a fine idea," Niles said, "so long as you can persuade her to stop bobbing up and down whenever I
look at her. She makes me more seasick than even
when we crossed from England."

They arrived at Sir Augustus O'Banyon's white
and lemon-colored house just in good time for tea.
A pause to change Melinda's nappies and dress, and
the Alardyce family were escorted through and out
the rear of the graciously proportioned three-story
house.

At a table set outside, but complete with napery
and silver, Paige sat gazing over a peaceful view of gently moving river and tumbledown castle half in, half
above the water on the other side. Hearing their ap-
proach, she turned and began to rise. There was
something ungainly about her once slim figure.

Handing Melinda to Niles, Rose hurried down the
sloping lawn. "Why didn't you write to me?" she demanded, embracing her.

"Oh, I didn't know how to tell you. I don't know
what your parents are going to say. Having one's first
child at the same time one's brother is having grand-
children is a little strange."

"Not at all. What does Augustus say?"

"He pretends he expected this all along. But he
struts about like a peacock."

Niles had reached them, and Paige held out her
arms for Melinda. At first, the baby was shy, ducking
her head into her father's neck, but when the adults
laughed, she couldn't resist looking around. Within

half an hour, she was seated on Paige's lap, eating crackers.

"Where is Augustus?" Niles asked, trying to pretend an intense discussion of breast-feeding was not going on around him.

"He rode into Cork to meet the mail coach from . . . here he comes now."

Rose stood up to greet her uncle-by-marriage civilly. Instead, she gave a shriek of joy and ran up the slope to throw her arms around a tall handsome soldier walking at Augustus's side. "I declare I'm jealous," Niles said.

"As well you should be," Paige said knowingly. "My friends in Dublin write that he is quite the lover. Mothers are starting to look at him askance, since he is never serious."

"Does he do well in the service?" Niles asked, reaching for a macaroon and watching his wife and brother-in-law come toward them, arm-in-arm, chattering like magpies.

"Augustus's cronies say he's taken to it like an eagle to the sky. The colonel of his regiment is an old comrade and has quite taken Rupert under his wing."

"Look what Uncle Augustus has brought you, Melinda. Your very own uncle."

"B'Jove, is this Melinda? She doesn't take after her father, thank heaven."

"Watch your tone, my lad," Niles said. "I still have your vowels and might make demands."

"I thought Rose had persuaded you to throw those in the fire long since," Rupert said uncaringly. "Let me have her. I charm all the women these days."

Melinda was fascinated by the gold embroidery on his collar but soon grew sleepy from the long trip and the unaccustomed stimulation of five adult voices all talking at once. Rose carried her upstairs, directed by Paige's pretty Irish maid. The cool nursery was full of shadows from the tall trees filtering the westering sunlight. Best of all, there was no sign of Mrs. Jarricks. Rose gave a limp Melinda to Nancy, who was tidying away the mountains of essentials a baby needed to travel.

In her own room, a pleasantly white chamber one floor below, Rose looked in the mirror and shook her head. It was a measure of the love her family bore her, she supposed, that no one had mentioned how completely haggard she looked. After the application of soap and water and a thorough brushing of her hair, Rose lay down beneath the white coverlet on the dark four-poster bed. She promised herself she'd sleep for only a few minutes.

When she awoke, it was full dark and someone was coming in. "Lucy?" Rose asked.

"No, it's me." Niles closed the door behind him with his foot and crossed the floor, balancing a tray and a candle. "You've slept through dinner," he said, "so I brought you some."

"Thank you, darling," she said. "But you should have wakened me."

"I did try. However, I didn't have a brass band ready and I wouldn't let Rupert try. He had some clever notions . . ."

"He always does."

Niles put the tray across her knees and sat down to talk to her while she ate. The soft candlelight brought out the gleams in her cascading hair and made her pupils huge and dark. He knew the texture of her velvet skin so well that he could remember the softness without touching her. Niles marveled they'd been two years married and he still desired her as passionately as on that first night.

When she finished, she stretched luxuriously, her arms above her head. Niles took the tray from her lap and put it outside the door. When the lock clicked, Rose smiled invitingly. "I should check on the nursery," she said.

"I did. All's well."

"All's well," she repeated as Niles came into her arms.

Historical Romance from
Jo Ann Ferguson